AN AMISH HERITAGE

TERRI DOWNES

An Amish Heritage

Terri Downes

Published by Trellis Publishing, 2021.

AN AMISH HERITAGE

First edition. July 3, 2021.

Copyright © 2021 Terri Downes.

ISBN: 979-8224013395

Written by Terri Downes.

"Good afternoon, everyone. My name is Mary Lancaster, and this is my heritage presentation."

Mary paused and looked up from her notes with a slight frown on her face.

"I know you all already know that, but that's how I started when I did this at school."

"We know. Go on, sweetie," said her father, smiling.

Mary nodded and looked back at her notes.

"I would like to begin by thanking two people. The first is my grandfather, Abraham, whose stories helped me to write this report."

Abraham beamed from his easy chair, set up in a sunny corner at the back of the living room.

"And secondly, I would like to thank Michael Stoltzfus, who convinced him to tell me the whole story."

***

"So this is your granddaughter, Abraham," said Michael. "She looks like you."

He smiled down at the serious-faced little girl at the kitchen table in Abraham's small kitchen. She had the same wide blue eyes as the old man who sat opposite her, and his slightly snub nose.

"She looks more like her father," said Abraham, referring to his son. "She's here doing a project for school."

"I need some stories about my family history," explained Mary. "My teacher was really interested when I told her that a lot of my family was Amish. Are you Amish as well?"

Michael nodded.

"You can tell from the clothing," said Abraham. "Remember I told you about the special clothes we wear?"

"Oh yeah, with the suspenders, I see. And what about the women? The hats and all?"

"I guess it might be better to speak to one of the ladies about that," said Abraham, scratching his head. "Maybe we could arrange to have you talk to one of them. Say, Michael, are you still riding with the Miller girl these days?"

Michael felt a blush rising to his cheeks.

"Uh, no, not these days, no," he said hesitantly.

Abraham frowned.

"That's a shame, I thought..." he trailed off, leaving an awkward pause to fill the room for a moment.

"So you have dating and stuff here, then?" piped up Mary, her head still buried in her notes.

Michael walked past her toward the kitchen counter, to put down the groceries he had brought for Abraham and also in the hopes that he could hide his flaming face. It seemed that nine-year-olds in *Englisch* households weren't taught when not to ask a question.

"We do. It's usually different to what you would think of as dating," said her grandfather. "Right, Michael?"

Michael scowled at Abraham behind Mary's head. His family had been close with Abraham ever since the older man had moved back to the community after living in the *Englisch* world for three decades. Michael had been taking care of him for a while, and Abraham often treated him as something of a son – complete with the notion that he should be able to tease him about any subject he wanted.

Michael was about to excuse himself, when Mary spoke once more.

"What about your wife, grandpa? She was also Amish, right? How did you two meet?"

At this, Michael halted.

He had never heard Abraham speak about his wife. He knew that Rebecca had indeed been Amish, like Abraham, and that they had left the community at the same time. Any other parts of the story had been left untold, however. If anyone ever brought it up, Abraham would quickly change the subject.

Once, when one of Michael's sisters had pushed a little too hard, convinced that she could make Abraham tell her the story, Michael had come across Abraham later – he had been crying. Michael had made sure that none of his siblings ever mentioned the subject again.

He kept his gaze on Abraham, wondering if he should say something, or distract Mary somehow. But Abraham was looking at his granddaughter with a strange expression on his face. It was gentle, as though he were seeing someone else where she sat.

"You don't have to say," Mary said, a little shyly, as the silence stretched on. "I just... my dad was never able to talk to me about it, and I always wondered. But I guess maybe that means it's a secret?"

Perhaps she did have some awareness of when to keep things quiet, reflected Michael.

"No, I..." Abraham smiled a little. "I guess I can tell you a little bit. But I'm afraid it won't be very helpful for your project. See, although Rebecca and I were both Amish, we didn't meet in the community."

"You didn't?" Michael spoke without thinking.

Abraham looked at him, a suggestion of laughter playing about his eyes.

"No," he said. "We didn't."

***

Two months into his course at Elmsfield college, and Abraham had been almost completely convinced that he would be joining the *Englisch* world after he graduated. He was not sure how to tell his family – although they may have already begun to suspect. They would have noticed that he was spending more and more time on the campus, and less time at home. They would no doubt have also noticed that the clothes he left and came home in every day were never dirty, due to the fact that he was changing into more modern clothing for his classes.

Many of the Amish youth did the same thing, to the point that it was often impossible to know whether or not another student was Amish until you heard them speak.

When Abraham saw Rebecca for the first time, he thought that she was *Englisch*. She was dressed very modestly, in a long skirt and high necked sweater, but otherwise looked like many of the other girls from *Englisch* farming families. Well, at least to the casual observer. To Abraham, she looked like nothing he had ever seen before.

He spotted her while walking through the grassy quad at the center of the campus one afternoon. He had been talking with a friend, and had completely lost his train of thought as Rebecca had crossed ahead of them.

She was walking with confidence, head high, laughing at something a friend of hers was saying. She looked like a ray of sunshine floating across the quad.

Abraham had not heard one word of the class that followed. Afterward, he had walked back through the quad, looking left and right in desperation, trying to spot the golden girl from before.

He had entirely failed to look in front, however, and had tripped right over a bag that someone had left lying on the ground. Having landed sprawled across the grass, he decided to lie there for a while and berate himself for his idiocy until the friend who had been walking with him managed to stop laughing.

It was then that he had heard footsteps beside him, and a voice, with a very slight Dutch accent.

"Are you all right?" it had said.

Somehow, he had known who was speaking before he had even looked up.

***

"You can't just leave it there," said Michael. "You're going to have to give her more than that, or she'll die of curiosity."

"You mean you will," said Abraham, pretending to swat at the younger man.

"I'd like to hear more if I can, grandpa," said Mary, gathering her things. "But you can decide what to say. And I have a lot of other questions I didn't get to yet – is it okay for me to come back later in the week?"

"That'll be just fine," smiled Abraham. "If you don't find it too dull."

"No, I like it here," said Mary, although her tone seemed to suggest that she was not entirely sure why she liked it.

"Well then. Why don't I have this busybody here walk you to your bus stop?"

Michael prepared to stand from where he had been sitting at the kitchen table. He had not meant to become so enraptured in the story, but he had not been able to help himself.

"It's okay, there was a nice lady who walked me over before – my mom knows her from the market. She's going to walk me back now, she's meeting me out front."

"If you say so."

Michael followed Abraham to the porch to wave goodbye to Mary.

Within seconds, he wished that he hadn't.

"Is that…?"

Abraham squinted at the figure who greeted Mary at the road side and took her book bag from her. Tall, dark haired, willowy – someone Michael would have recognized from a mile away.

Michael swallowed.

"Yes, that's Hannah," he confirmed.

"The Miller girl," said Abraham, sounding curious.

"Yes," said Michael shortly.

"The one you were seeing."

"That's the one."

"But you aren't seeing her any more?"

"No."

"Because...?"

"Because."

Michael could feel Abraham's disapproving gaze as he stood looking at Hannah, who had not seen him, beginning to walk away with Mary.

"Why not?" asked Abraham.

Michael sighed.

"Because... it's complicated."

"I'm pretty smart, you know, I could probably keep up."

"I just..." Michael looked up toward the sky for a moment, wondering how on earth he was supposed to put into words something he did not quite understand himself.

"Weren't you two always good friends?" prompted Abraham. "Did something happen?"

"No, nothing happened. I guess that's..." Michael pressed his lips together for a moment. "I guess that's the problem. It wasn't... like you meeting Rebecca. It wasn't meeting someone and just *knowing*. That was always something I wanted. But with me and Hannah, it was more like it was just expected, you know? Like it was just the most sensible thing to do. That's not how I want to find love."

Abraham huffed out a sigh.

"That's not quite how it was, Michael."

"Oh, no?" Michael could not help but smirk a little. "Maybe you should tell the rest of the story so I can find out for myself."

"Brat."

Michael laughed.

"And you're also an idiot," added the older man, as he turned to go back inside.

"Why's that?"

"Because you haven't looked away from that road once since you saw Hannah standing on it."

***

Neither Rebecca nor Abraham had brought up the fact that they were both Amish during their first conversation. It had almost been as though they had agreed beforehand to ignore the fact. They talked instead of their courses at the college, and the friends they had made.

They got halfway through their second conversation, over sodas at the college cafeteria, before the subject was finally broached; Abraham asked Rebecca what she was planning to do after she graduated.

She laughed shortly and raised an eyebrow at him.

"There's a question I'm not getting asked a lot," she said. "My family seem to be afraid of the answer."

"You're thinking of leaving the People," surmised Abraham.

Rebecca nodded.

"You?" she asked.

"I guess. It's difficult, you know?"

"I do know."

The conversation had fallen onto new lines, then, about family and obligation and doing the right thing. Neither of them had tried to convince the other to stay or to go – again, it seemed almost as though the allowed topics had been decided on before they had begun speaking.

Abraham had known, even then, that a relationship with Rebecca would make an already complicated decision even more complicated. If one of them stayed, and the other left, then there was no way that they could be together. It might be safer to decide now, rather than wait for heartbreak later. Yet that was a huge commitment to make just as they were starting to get to know one another.

In the end, they had not said anything about it.

***

Michael tried to stay patient as Mary interrupted yet again, with a new question about the rules that Abraham kept referring to. He reminded himself that the whole point of this story was for her school project, and that he should consider himself lucky to get to sit in on the interview.

On the other hand, he already knew the rules surrounding the *Ordnung*, baptism and the like, and he was eager to hear more about Abraham's budding romance.

He kept his peace, however, and went to refill everyone's glasses with iced tea while Abraham explained himself. The afternoon was growing hot, and the cool drinks were much needed.

Michael had done his best not to let Abraham catch his eye as he told the story. The older man had been teasing him about Hannah ever since he had glimpsed her on the road. And Michael – well, he had been thinking. Hard. Perhaps there had been something there that he had missed. Maybe Hannah was meant to be his destiny after all.

Although if she was, then he was not sure what to do about it. He had been the one to break things off. She had seemed to understand when he had explained that he did not want them to end up together for no better reason than proximity. She had even agreed when he suggested that they would be able to remain good friends. Yet she had managed to avoid him ever since.

How on earth could he approach her again? Michael stared into the refrigerator for a while, as though the eggs might be able to give him an answer, but was left as clueless as before.

By the time he returned, Abraham was ready to begin again.

***

Rebecca swore that she had not been the one to tell her family that she had been spending time with Abraham. Abraham, for his part, had no idea who had informed his family of the same fact.

Perhaps it did not matter how they had found out – the fact remained that they had, and both sides were unbearably pleased about it.

"What do you mean *unbearably*?" Abraham had asked, when Rebecca had said this.

"I mean it's hard enough trying to work all of this out without having to worry about disappointing my family," Rebecca had scowled, aiming a kick at a pile of snow as they walked through a small park near the college.

They had been spending all of their time together at the college, or at the park, or even at the small diners and cafes that littered the neighborhood and preyed on students who needed immediate sustenance after studying themselves dizzy. They had not gone riding or walking together in the way that they would have at home. They had not told their parents of their relationship.

Abraham had panicked when his mother had come to him and said how pleased she was that he was seeing an Amish girl, and how much she looked forward to the two of them settling down in the community together after all of this school business was finished with. He had claimed that Rebecca was just a friend.

He had felt bad about this, as Rebecca was definitely more than a friend, but Rebecca had apparently had the same reaction when her parents brought up the subject.

"What are we going to do?" Abraham had wondered aloud.

"Let's not think about it right now," Rebecca had suggested.

Abraham had tried to insist that they come up with some sort of plan – but then Rebecca had thrown a snowball at him and things had become very distracting.

***

"I thought you said you wanted to leave? Why not just go together?" asked Mary.

"We both knew what we wanted – to learn and work in the bigger world. I wanted to be a teacher, and Rebecca wanted to work for a charity. But we also didn't want to leave our families, or our homes. It's a connection you can't break – you feel it, all the time," said her grandfather. He tapped his chest, just over his heart. "In here."

His voice wavered for a moment, and he drew out his handkerchief.

Mary, who Michael now knew to have a great deal more sensitivity than he had given her credit for, moved over to her grandfather and patted his hand as it lay on the armrest of his easy chair.

Sensing that this was a private moment, Michael cleared the tea glasses quietly and went to carry them back into the kitchen. He did not get further than the hall, however, halting as the front door opened.

Hannah stopped dead when she saw him.

She might have been about to say hello, but Michael quickly motioned for her to be quiet and follow him. She obliged, walking past the closed door of the living room.

"I came to fetch Mary," she said quietly, as soon as they reached the kitchen. "What's going on?"

"Abraham's telling her a story about her grandma," said Michael, placing the glasses in the sink. "He got kind of emotional."

"Oh." Hannah rocked back on her heels for a moment, nodding in understanding.

Michael leaned against the counter and looked at her. It was not as though there was any reason for her to look different to when they had last spoken, but after that sudden moment of reconsideration the other day, he had imagined that perhaps the next time he saw her he would be stricken with her beauty. In truth, she was not as beautiful as many other girls in the area. Not that she was unattractive – but Michael had not had any competition when he had first asked her to drive. She was fully aware of this herself, and had even joked about it a couple of times.

She did not look ready to make any jokes now, however.

He had been thinking about her so much, recently, imagining a dozen different scenarios for when they would speak. Now that it was happening, he could not think of what to say.

Was he in love with her? He had hoped that it would be obvious when they were up close like this, that he would feel the way that Abraham had described in his stories. But all he could see was his friend.

"Is Mary emotional as well?" she asked. "You know I'm not so great with that kind of thing."

"I think she's all right," said Michael.

"How come you're getting to hear the story, anyhow?" asked Hannah, smiling a little. "Doesn't seem fair, after you forbade everyone else from bringing it up."

"Mary brought it up," protested Michael, laughing. "I happened to be there. And you know I like a good love story."

But at this, Hannah's face fell.

"I know," she said, trying to gather her smile back up as Michael gazed at her.

"Hannah," he said hesitantly, "are you... are you upset about what happened?"

It was a dangerous question to ask, Michael knew, and not well phrased. But he had forgotten all of the far better questions that he had scripted in his imagination for this moment.

Sure enough, Hannah frowned.

"Of course I was upset," she said. "Why would you ask that?"

"I just meant – I know it wasn't all that great, what happened, and I've been thinking about it. I guess I just kind of realized that I hadn't thought it through."

This was really not going the way that he had hoped, Michael thought, as Hannah's frown deepened. Why was he always so much better at talking to people in his head?

But there was nothing for it now. Already, Hannah looked as though she was beginning to understand what Michael was trying to say.

"I may have made a hasty decision, is the thing," he said. "And if you wanted to try again..."

Hannah stared at Michael for a moment. The she closed her eyes and raised her hands to her face.

"Are you joking," she said flatly, speaking through her fingers. "You've got to be joking."

Michael swallowed nervously.

"Uh – no, I'm not –"

"You broke things off," said Hannah, speaking calmly and deliberately, "because you weren't in love with me. Remember? You care about me but you're not in love with me?"

Michael blinked for a moment as Hannah brought her hands back down and stared at him. He had forgotten that he had said that to her.

"So are you saying that's changed suddenly? You feel differently?"

She did not sound as though she was expecting a *yes*. Michael cringed.

"Well, not exactly different, but..."

"Michael." Hannah held up one hand. "You ended things because you wanted some grand, sweeping romance, and I wasn't the one who could give that to you. And I'm still not. If you're somehow hoping that I've become a different person since the last time you saw me, you're going to be very disappointed."

None of the conversations that Michael had imagined had gone this route. As he floundered for something to say, he heard the door to the living room open. Before he could think of a way to keep her, Hannah had turned and walked back into the hall.

He heard her greeting Mary and Abraham, her voice cheerful and light. She seemed to be very good at hiding her feelings.

He wondered how many of them she had hidden from him.

"Michael?" called Mary from the hall. "Are you coming to hear more?"

Michael stepped into the hall, which now felt a little crowded with four people in the tiny space.

"I thought you were leaving?" he asked Mary.

He nodded vaguely at Hannah, who was not looking at him.

"My mom called," said Mary, "and asked if I could take the later bus. Grandpa says he can tell some more of the story."

"Are you sure?" asked Michael doubtfully, looking at his friend.

Abraham's eyes, however, were bright and clear. He seemed suddenly eager to delve back into his past.

"Sure as can be," he said. "Let's settle back in. Hannah, you'll stay too?"

The question was thrown out casually, and it took a moment for Michael to realize what Abraham was doing. He wanted to signal to Abraham that this was a bad idea, but the space was too small to get away with it.

"Ah... it's all right, I can come back when it's time for the next bus," said Hannah.

"But you'll have to walk all the way home and just turn around again," said Abraham. "Rest up a little, go on."

He smiled encouragingly, and ushered Mary and Hannah into the sitting room. Michael hesitated in the doorway, thinking that he should escape somehow, but was forced into the room by a not so gentle push from Abraham.

Michael sat down, and began imagining the many things that he would say to Abraham when this was over.

***

The decision that Abraham and Rebecca made did not happen quickly. It took a lot of discussion deliberation, with both of them debating each side several times. Eventually, however, they brought their relationship to a cordial close, celebrating their mutual freedom with a milkshake each at one of their favorite diners.

"At least I can be honest with my folks now," Rebecca had sighed. "My grandma will be disappointed, but hopefully she'll stop hinting about how nice I'd look in a blue wedding dress."

Abraham wished that she would be more sad about it, but he had to admit that he was also feeling relieved. Now he could focus on qualifying as a teacher without worrying about everything else at the same time.

"You would," he smiled. "But you can get your own blue dress, without the wedding."

"I might just do that."

***

"You broke up?"

"Yes. It was the best thing we could have done."

Michael and Mary both stared at Abraham as though he had announced that he was about to perform a handstand. Michael felt completely floored by this revelation, and had temporarily forgotten his irritation at Abraham.

He had thought that Abraham had been telling the perfect love story. A predestined meeting, love at first sight, a hidden romance that would overcome its challenges. If there was to be a breaking off, it should have been over something big, something that would eventually lead to both of them realizing their mistake and running back into each other's arms. This did not fit.

"We weren't ready to admit how much we needed one another," Abraham said. "We loved each other, sure, but we were young. We thought that inconvenience meant that we weren't meant for one another. We didn't know what real love was."

"But you did end up together anyway though. Did you still think that maybe you would, when you broke up?" asked Mary.

"I don't think I did," said Abraham, shaking his head. "But what I knew didn't matter. It was like I said before –" he tapped his heart again. "We were connected. We couldn't break it even when we tried. And we did try."

Abraham began to talk about the other girls that he went out after the breakup – a few from college, and a few from his home community. Mary then had several questions to ask about the process of Amish dating, which Abraham was happy to explain.

Mary seemed strangely entranced by the idea of such a careful courtship. She mentioned that she had always thought the stories of her own parents' romance were unusually old fashioned. Presumably, Abraham and Rebecca had raised their children to high standards even away from Amish rules.

Hannah and Michael remained seated in silence for the duration of the questioning. Michael wondered if Hannah, like him, was being far too directly reminded of the time they had spent together. The long rides, the walks, the evenings talking by the fire.

No doubt Abraham had planned this, thinking that he might be able to bring the couple back together. Michael felt mortified at the entire situation, not least because of the words that Abraham had spoken regarding himself and Rebecca.

Was it truly possible to miss love when it was right there in front of you? Could he himself be missing something so important?

Michael risked a glance at Hannah as she sat leaning a little toward the open window, trying to catch the evening breeze. He still felt no differently toward her – but why, then, was he still thinking about her?

Despite the stricken silence from both Michael and Hannah, Abraham seemed to be under the impression that the hour of storytelling had been a great success. As Hannah was leaving with Mary, he made a point of inviting her to sit in to hear the rest the next time Mary visited.

"We're nearly done, I think," he said. "I've answered all of the practical questions. All we have to do is finish the story."

"Sure, that would be nice," said Hannah.

She smiled politely, then stepped out onto the porch to wait as Mary collected her papers and shoes. Michael followed her, waiting until Mary and Abraham were out of earshot before he spoke.

"You don't have to," he said. "He'll understand – and I can talk to him."

Hannah looked only briefly over at Michael before returning her attention to the sunset blush settling over the garden.

"Why wouldn't I want to hear the end?" she asked. "Mary's been filling me in since the start. I've been wishing I could hear it for myself for ages."

"Oh." Michael glanced down at his feet. "Well, I guess I can come another time to get the end for myself then."

"What are you talking about?" frowned Hannah.

"I thought..." Michael hesitated. "I thought maybe you'd want me to stay away for a while, or..."

"Don't be ridiculous. We can both hear the story."

"Oh. Good, all right then." Michael nodded. "It's just I figured I made you uncomfortable, before. You know."

Hannah sighed deeply.

"Of course you did. It's not nice to be reminded that I don't fit into your notions of romance, Michael, but I already knew that. I can't go getting upset every time I think about it."

"It's not just about romance," Michael started, knowing even as he did so that it was probably a bad idea. "It's about – what Abraham said. A connection."

It had definitely been a bad idea. Hannah turned her head away with a jerk.

"Maybe if I'd been prettier you would have felt a connection," she muttered.

"What?" said Michael, taking a small step backward.

Hannah shot him a glance, then pressed her hands over her face again.

"I'm sorry," she said. "That was unfair."

"It – it's all right," he said, although he could not say anything else to her.

He could not say anything at all, not even to Abraham, who persisted in looking annoyingly smug as he watched the two girls walking back down the road.

"It's just the one part left," Abraham said quietly, when he finally turned to go back into the house. "It's where things get a little complicated; but I don't think I could stop once I started. I have to get to the end."

Michael nodded, only half paying attention; his thoughts were still trailing after Hannah, walking away from him once more.

***

The story did, indeed, become complicated. Because, despite all of his intentions of leaving the fold and striking out on his own, Abraham had eventually found himself thinking about staying at home. He began to spend more time back at the community in the evenings and on weekends, and asked more Amish girls to drive than he did *Englisch* girls to go walking with him.

Rebecca, on the other hand, was making waves at the college, getting ready to graduate early and head off to a job offer in another state. Abraham knew about this before she told her family; they had not been together for a while by that point, and he was only able to offer her a nod of encouragement across a crowded lunch table when he heard the news.

The following day, however, he had been at home, working on some project or other in the barn, half-listening to some old argument being rehashed between two of his brothers, when he had suddenly felt the need to lay down his tools.

He had ignored his brothers' questions, and began to walk across the pasture behind the barn. When he had climbed over the fence into the next field, he had seen a lone figure walking toward him.

The sun had been behind her; he should not have been able to recognize her from that distance. But he ran the rest of the way anyway, knowing as he did exactly who he was running toward.

Rebecca had been in tears. She had told her family; she had hoped that they would understand. They had not.

She had begged, they had refused to listen. They had been angry. Their anger was due to their love for her, and their fear that she was making the wrong decision, but these facts had not changed anything. The Rebecca that Abraham met in the fields that day was different than she had been before. Her heart had been broken.

They sat on the fence together and spoke as they had not done in a long time.

Abraham asked, tentatively, whether Rebecca might change her decision. But she could not. And even if she did stay, she said, she was not sure if it would be the same. She had never seen her family like this before.

"The way my mother looked at me," she said, shivering in the warm afternoon sun. "I don't think I could speak to her again without remembering that expression. Like I was a stranger to her."

The longer they talked, the more sure Abraham became of what he needed to do. Rebecca did not once ask anything of him, for his help or support. She had heard of his decision to commit to the People following his graduation from college, and would never have asked him to change his mind for her. But she looked at him, and he could not look away, nor move.

Eventually, they had fallen silent, side by side.

"I'm afraid my parents are going to be very angry with me as well," Abraham had said.

Rebecca had sobbed anew when she had realized what he was saying. But as her tears fell, she also managed to smile.

***

"I had always looked forward to getting married," Abraham said wistfully.

He stared at the fireplace, left empty in the heat of the warm fall evening. Michael, Mary and Hannah sat nearby, each forgetting themselves as they leaned forward into the story. Mary had let her pencil drop. It did not matter; this was something she would not forget.

"But it was quiet, in the end. Some friends from college acted as witnesses. We stayed in various people's guest rooms for a few months. We didn't even get much of a honeymoon, as we were studying for finals. But I couldn't regret it, not even for a second, no matter how sad we were."

"You missed it here," said Mary quietly.

"We both did." Abraham sighed. "We lived as simply as we could, even when we moved across the country for Rebecca's work. We'd talk about the old days, sometimes."

"Even after grandma's family were so mean about everything?" asked Mary, frowning.

"They weren't mean," said her grandfather, softly. "They wanted the best for her. They loved her. And besides – it wasn't about them, not really. It was the place, the People, the community, everything. You can't get away from these things."

"The connection," Mary said.

"Exactly."

Wordlessly, Mary raised her hand in the same way that Abraham had done before, and touched the spot above her heart.

"That's why you came back?" she asked.

"I came back for Rebecca," said Abraham. "We had thirty wonderful years together, in the end. But even after your father and your uncles were grown, Rebecca never felt that she would be able to return here. But after she passed, I couldn't stay away. She would have liked to know I came back, I think."

Abraham's eyes were once more streaming with tears, but this time he did not stem them. Mary went again to his side, as before, this time with her own eyes sparkling wet.

Michael decided that he should also follow the pattern that had previously been set and remove himself – but when he turned to indicate to Hannah that they should both step out, he saw that she was already gone.

He frowned, and walked out into the hallway and onto the front porch, but she was nowhere in sight. He began to feel nervous. Was something wrong?

Maybe he should just leave her be, wherever she went. She had already confirmed that he had been making her uncomfortable with his renewed attentions.

Michael blushed a little, remembering – especially in light of Abraham's finished story. He thought of Abraham, walking away into the unknown, but still sure of what he was going to find. What were Michael's half-hearted attempts compared with that? How could he have convinced himself that he was destined for some great love when he was not willing to show the commitment it took to test it?

Provided, of course, that he did love her, Michael thought, as he walked back through the hallway and into the kitchen. He may have been humbled and made aware of his ignorance, but that only made things more uncertain. Abraham, at the very least, had known how he felt when the moment arrived. How was Michael supposed to recognize love when it came?

This was the last thought that passed through his mind as he stepped out of the kitchen door. He had intended to glance around the tiny back porch and see if Hannah had stepped out for some air, and perhaps ask her to make tea.

She was there – but he did not speak to her, not right away. She, too, was crying.

She was leaning with both hands on the railing in front of her, facing out into the back yard. Tears rolled down her cheeks, and her eyes were wide as she stared out into the mellow light of evening. It only took a moment for her to realize that Michael was there, however, and she quickly turned away, reaching into a pocket for her handkerchief.

"Sorry," she said thickly. "That ending really got to me. I must look a mess."

"You look beautiful."

Michael was not sure whether he realized the truth of the words as he said them, or if his sudden understanding forced them out of his mouth. But he was certain that he had never meant anything he had said in his life quite so strongly.

Hannah did not seem to understand this; she rolled her eyes slightly, as though she thought he was joking, or being overly polite.

"No, I mean it."

Michael felt his chest tighten as Hannah still refused to look at him, dabbing at her eyes determinedly. How had he not seen her before? How had he not recognized her?

"Hannah, you are. You are so beautiful. I don't – I don't know how to –"

What could he possibly say? Michael walked over to stand as close to Hannah as he dared, keeping his eyes on hers as he did so. They were still shining wet, and her cheeks were in bright contrast with her pale face. He could not look away.

Hannah looked back, her expression moving from uncertainty to active doubt.

"Michael, you already –"

"No, I know."

Michael had brought up the subject already, and been rebuffed. But that had been lazy, a low effort suggestion riding on the fantasy of a love that would simply fall into place. This was different.

"And I told you, nothing's changed," said Hannah. "So..."

Michael shook his head. He did not know how to explain what he felt without sounding as though he were making another idiotic assumption. He did not have any words for a moment like this.

So instead of speaking, he slowly raised his hand. And tapped his chest. Just over his heart.

Hannah followed the moment with her eyes. They were brimming over once more with tears when she raised her gaze to meet Michael's.

Michael was still trying to think of something to say when she unexpectedly smiled, one eyebrow quirking upward.

"Don't you start crying as well, now," she said.

Michael moved his hands to his face, where he was surprised to find that tears had indeed begun to fall. He reached for his own handkerchief, but was unable to muster even a fraction of the embarrassment that he would normally feel over shedding public tears.

"I think I'm just crying because you're crying," he said.

"But I'm only crying because Abraham and Mary were crying," protested Hannah. "Or that's what got me started, anyway."

"You're saying I had nothing to do with it? I'm offended," said Michael.

"You're ridiculous," said Hannah.

"I know." Michael leaned back against the railing. "And I'm an idiot."

Hannah laughed.

"No, I really am. I already made such a mess of this – twice. I don't know how you put up with me."

"Neither do I," said Hannah, folding her handkerchief and putting it away.

Michael hesitated for a moment.

"But... but you will though, won't you?" he asked.

"Put up with you, you mean?"

Hannah smiled. Her hand moved upward, almost as though she were not thinking about it, until it was laid over her heart.

"Yes, I think I will."

****

"That concludes the narrative section of my presentation. If you –"

Mary broke off once more and looked around the room again. The fall light had shifted as she was speaking; she had not noticed, so carefully had she been following her notes. She had not wanted to miss a single piece of her grandfather's story.

Her audience remained still, waiting for her to continue.

"This was the part where I used the visual aids and answered questions about the laws and everything," she explained, "except you all know that stuff already. So... I guess I'll just skip to the end, if that's all right?"

"It's your presentation," said Hannah, smiling from her seat next to Michael.

"But it's your present," Mary reminded her.

It had been a strange wedding present to ask for, she thought, especially considering that her mom had offered to give Mary money to buy something really good. But they had wanted to hear her report. True, it had gotten her an A+ last week at the end of term. Maybe Abraham had told them that – he had been very proud when he had heard – and they had wanted to experience it in person.

"Just finish the way you did in class," prompted Michael.

"Well – okay. So I guess what I learned from this project was that heritage is a difficult thing. It's about belonging to a place, but also about the people that you share it with. And sometimes you have to choose one or the other. But you'll always belong, no matter what..."

Mary looked up and caught her grandfather's eye; he was smiling. She imagined Rebecca sitting next to him, with her own golden smile and laughing eyes.

"...And you'll always know when you're home."

UNCOMMON AMISH GROUND

MONICA MARKS

"Father, please don't –!"

The plea came too late and was unheeded as a bucket of cold water was released onto Emilia's head, about her bonnet and down along the front of her dress.

"Father!" she screamed, furiously. "Why on earth would you do such a thing!"

Jumping from her chair, she whirled around to face him, her brown eyes flashing with anger. To her dismay, he was beaming as if he had bestowed some act of kindness upon her.

"Emilia, it is summertime! You are cooped up within the walls of a house, knitting a sweater," he replied, reaching out to take her arm. "I do believe that the sunshine is calling your name."

"A sweater that is now ruined!" Emilia complained but allowed for Abel to lead her from the dark stone house into the yard, dripping water heavily along the way. Her two younger sisters were engaged in a game of hopscotch on the road, their long braids flailing in the wind.

"You see? Even the children know better than to stay indoors when the day is fraught with beauty. What kind of example are you setting for the young ones?"

"Father, I do not have time for trivial tasks. I needed to have that sweater finished for the marketplace. After which I have to begin making supper. Now I will be up half the night knitting!"

"Ah! One less sweater at the marketplace will not be the end of days. Also, you do not have to make supper tonight. We have been invited to the home of our neighbor." Emilia turned and looked at him suspiciously at the sudden announcement.

"Which neighbor?" she demanded. Again, Abel smiled, undaunted by his eldest daughter's scrutiny.

"The new members of our community. They reside only a few houses down the road."

"Father, you don't mean that sour faced man with the sullen little girl, do you? I did not like the looks of those two at church. They seem to not like being here. We don't know anything about them."

"My dear, you do not like the look of anyone. That is because you don't truly look at anyone. And that is why we are going this evening; to learn about them and make them feel welcome. "

"Oh father, that is simply not accurate. I do not engage in silliness like other women. I much prefer my own company to idle chit chat. There is no harm in that. I believe it shows that I have a strong head on my shoulders."

"Indeed, it does, my daughter. Once in a while, however, you can relax and enjoy the sunshine." Emilia did not reply. This was an old argument. Since the passing of her mother six years earlier, Abel Troyer had done his best to keep his three daughters in high spirits. The two youngest had eventually moved on from the unexpected death but Emilia had clung to the memory of her mother like a spider web shawl, refusing to let light into her life. Abel desperately missed the infectious sound of Emilia's laughter, a tone which used to ring through the hills of their community like a tinkling bell.

"Regardless, father, I see no reason why we should join Mr. Bawell and his daughter for supper," Emilia finally said. "But if you feel you must, by all means, do go without me."

"It is my wish that we attend supper at their residence and so we shall. I am still the head of this household, Emilia. I do not appreciate being contradicted." Abel was beginning to lose his good humor. He did not understand why everything had to be a fight with Emilia. When his wife had been alive, Emilia had been the model child, obedient and respectful. He knew she only wanted to be left alone to her brooding but he would not have it. She was perfectly healthy, a lovely, kind hearted woman who deserved happiness. It was his job as her father to ensure that she received it. Emilia wisely closed her mouth and turned to face her siblings as her father walked off into the back part of the yard, seeming to have no more interest in teasing his child.

"Emmy, will you play with us?" Collette called, her blonde hair almost white in the droplets of sunlight. Emilia forced herself to smile and shook her head. For a fleeting moment, she was tempted to join the children but she pushed the thought from her mind.

"Not today, Collette. I have work to do."

"You always have work to do, Emmy!" Evelyn pouted. Collette took her younger sister's hand and pulled the nine-year-old toward the veranda.

"She is busy taking care of us, Evie. We are going to mammi and dawdy's now anyway. We must get dressed."

"Wait one moment, Collette. You're going to mammi and dawdy's house? Father just said that we are going to our new neighbor's for supper. Are you certain?"

Collette paused at the door to allow Evelyn to pass.

"You and papa are going to Aaron Bawell's for supper. Evie and I are going to mammi and dawdy's." The girls disappeared into the house and Emilia was left on the porch, still dripping from her father's cold water bath. She narrowed her smoky eyes. *Why is he sending Evie and Collette to our grandparents' house? What is papa up to?* She cringed inwardly as she had her suspicions.

"Emilia, why do you insist on being so stubborn?"

"What is it, father? What have I done now?"

Abel sighed heavily and stared at his daughter as she descended the stairs from her bedroom.

"You know full well that you cannot attend this supper wearing working clothes. Please change into more appropriate attire." Emilia blinked her solemn eyes at him.

"But father, I believed this to be work." Abel scowled and pointed firmly up the staircase.

"You will do as I say immediately, Emilia. And that is quite enough of your impudence for one day." Emilia hung her head in shame, immediately reading her father's anger and slightly stung by his words. Abel was not one to raise his voice in anger.

"Yes father. I'm sorry." She hurried back up to change her clothes and wondered why she had performed such a defiant act. She knew that her father would not have allowed her to visit the Bawell house dressed in rags. It was disrespectful. Lately she had been feeling more and more feisty and if she was not already well into her late twenties, she would have thought that she was due to experience rumspringa. She had briefly experimented with cigarettes and beer when she was younger but she had since been baptized and was very happy in the community. Well, as happy as Emilia could be. There was an unsurmountable void which had filled Emilia since the death of her young mother. She was eternally grateful for the consistency and love given by Abel, however, Emilia and her mother had a bond that seemed to outlive death. Time did not heal her pain and eventually Emilia had succumbed to the fact that she was destined to be discontent for the remainder of her life. Yet lately, the sorrow had turned into some sort of boiling anger and no matter how Emilia tried, she could not seem to tame the beast which was growing within her.

Moments later, she was descending the stairs in a freshly ironed dark blue dress, a starch white bonnet covering her thick head of hair. Abel beamed happily.

"You look lovely. Much better. Shall we?" He offered his arm to his daughter and they started out the door.

"Father, why have you sent the children to mammi and dawdy's this evening?"

"Ah because this evening is for the older people, my dear daughter." Emilia swallowed a knowing grunt but said nothing. As they strolled up the walkway toward the Bawell household, the front door flew open and Emilia was facing the petulant stare of a six-year-old child. Her blue eyes looked like frosted panes of glass as she took in the sight of the two strangers on the porch.

"Good evening, Amity," Abel boomed amiably. "How are you this fine night?"

The girl did not respond and instead turned and disappeared out of view. Emilia gave her father a look but the older man did not meet her eyes. A moment later, Aaron Bawell appeared at the door.

"Please, come in," he said, extending the front door for them to enter. Abel smiled and nodding his thanks while Emilia reluctantly followed.

"May I introduce my daughter, Emilia?" Abel said, removing hat and gesturing toward Emilia.

"Yes," Aaron replied nodding and closing the door. Emilia was slightly taken aback by his disinterested response. In her grief, Emilia had not been interested in the prospect of marriage despite her father's endless prompting.

"It is not healthy for a woman to go through life without a companion, Emilia," Abel had told her countless times. "What of children?"

"I have two daughters in Evelyn and Collette," she had replied, only half jokingly. She had not the stomach to think of child bearing when her own mother had not had the chance to watch her daughters grow up. Eventually, Abel had forsaken the quest to marry off his oldest daughter. However, she had more callers than anyone else in her community and the reason for that was simple. She was the ideal wife. She was hard working, compassionate and a deep thinker. She possessed patience and everyone was a friend to her. Also, she was incredibly lovely, with long honey blonde hair and wide, innocent brown eyes, framed in long eyelashes. Whenever Emilia flashed an elusive smile, the entire world seemed to follow her lead. Even after years of rejecting suitor after suitor, they still came knocking on her door, eager to see her wed to them.

This is why Aaron Bawell's abrupt greeting was so stunning to Emilia. He was apparently unimpressed by Emilia's presence. *He does not know you,* Emilia reasoned, following the men into the sitting room. *He has only been in our district for two weeks. He has no reason to give you a second look.* Even as Emilia thought the words, she felt a strange pang of longing. She oddly wished him to look at her again. And again. *You must stop thinking this way!* She chided herself. *Your thoughts are that of a child in puppy love!* But Emilia could not stop staring at the newcomer and taking in all the details of his strong physique. His voice was deep and mellifluous and Emilia thought she could listen to him speak all day long. She felt a blush color her cheeks and she wondered what it was about Aaron which set him apart from the others who had bid for her hand in marriage. Certainly he was handsome but many men could claim the same. He donned a beard, an indication that he was married but there had been no mention of a mother for his young daughter. Emilia suddenly realized that she was very interested in learning more about the man in whose house she sat. Aaron and Abel were having a conversation of which Emilia heard none. As they finished speaking, Aaron looked about the room, somewhat confused.

"Amity!" Aaron called out. "Join us, please."

His demand was met with no response and sighing heavily after a moment, Aaron rose to his feet.

"Excuse me," he apologized before disappearing into the home. Emilia listened as his footsteps ascended up the staircase.

"Father, what on earth are we doing here?" Emilia asked, feeling distinctly uncomfortable. Abel gave her a sidelong look and smiled briefly.

"I believe you know what we are doing her, Emilia. Aaron Bawell is a successful carpenter. He is new to the community and has not been swayed by your endless rejection. He will be a perfect match for you."

"Father!" Emilia groaned. "I had hoped you had stopped with this matchmaking foolishness long ago."

"Emilia, it is not foolishness to want your children to be happy and begin a family. You are not going to be a young woman forever, child. You must consider your future."

"Father, I – "her words were cut short as Aaron returned to the sitting room, almost dragging along his daughter.

"Papa, I don't want them to be here," Amity Bawell snarled, glaring viciously at the strangers in her living room. Against the flickering kerosene lanterns, she almost looked diabolical, her small upper lip curled above her teeth, blue eyes aflame. She was otherwise a very pretty child, a spitting image of her father. She had long, straight black hair and cornflower blue eyes. Her features were softer, less defined than Aaron with his high cheekbones but she also had the extra fat of a small child.

"You will mind your manners!" Aaron snapped back, shooting an embarrassed look toward Abel.

"I do not like you!" Amity yelled, hands on her hips, addressing Emilia. Emilia was shocked by the defiance in the girl. She could not imagine either of her sisters ever speaking in such a way. *I don't believe I am overly fond of you either, little devil,* Emilia thought, narrowing her eyes at the child.

"Amity! You will stop this insolence immediately!" Aaron thundered, rising to his feet once more. "We are in the presence of guests. Your mother would be ashamed of your behavior!"

As if her father had physically struck her, Amity seemed to crumble to the floor. Her face went waxen and her eyes filled with tears. The deviousness evaporated and suddenly Emilia was staring at an ashen faced child. For a moment, she felt her heart crack. She had never seen a sorrier sight. Amity opened her mouth as if she were about to speak but no words fluttered from her small, pink lips. Then, tears streaked her chubby face and she ran, sobbing, from the room. Heavily, Aaron reclaimed his seat beside Abel. There was an awkward silence as everyone searched for the right words to speak. Finally, Abel cleared his throat, standing.

"We will call another time, Aaron," Emilia's father said magnanimously, ushering Emilia to her feet. "Young girls can have their bad days. I understand. I have three of them."

Abel put a smile to his statement to ease the younger man's discomfort but Aaron looked devastated, his deep blue eyes troubled and full.

"Every day is a bad day." He seemed to have heard the way his words sounded and he quickly rose to his feet.

"I apologize. I thought we had been here long enough for her to accept visitors. This transition has been extremely difficult on Amity." Aaron looked imploringly at Abel for understanding, completely ignoring Emilia. Inwardly she was shaking her head. *You are far too soft on the child. You should not make excuses,* Emilia thought. *These people are not the right fit for this community. We do not rear our children to act so recklessly.*

"Of course it has! She is but a small girl. She cannot be expected to understand so much change in so little time," Abel assured him. "Give her time."

"I will speak to the Bishop about her," Aaron promised, ushering them toward the door. "Once more, please forgive this disruption. I will reschedule our meal for another time."

"Please, do not worry. Perhaps next time you will visit with us. Evelyn is only a few years older than Amity. A friend may do her a world of good." Aaron looked thoughtful at the suggestion and nodded. The men bid each other adieu and Aaron closed the door in their wake without so much as a glance at Emilia. Again, she was stunned by his rudeness. Abel took Emilia's arm and guided her down the path leading to their modest house moments down the road. When she was quite sure they were out of earshot, Emilia turned to her father.

"Lord above, I have never seen such an ill behaved child in all of my life!" she exploded. "And that man, he's rude – "

"Emilia – "Abel attempted to cut her off but she was not finished.

"He barely spoke one full word to me. I see that the apple does not fall far from the tree! Can you imagine raising a child so willful – "

"Emilia – "

"And you, you father, why on God's green earth would you ever consider him a match for me?"

"Are you quite finished with your diatribe?" Abel asked tiredly, releasing her arm as they approached their house.

"You can't say that you weren't shocked at her behavior, father," Emilia said, baffled by his calm demeanor.

"I was not," Abel replied. Emilia arched an eyebrow, her brown eyes cynical.

"How not?"

"I was not surprised because you and your sisters behaved very similarly after your mother passed also." A wave of dizziness overwhelmed Emilia as his words set in, instantly followed by deep regret.

"You mean to tell me that Amity's mother has recently passed away?" she whispered.

"Yes. Not three weeks ago. That is why Aaron has uprooted his life and started fresh here. Amity could not bear to be in their home without her mother. He is doing his best for his daughter. You could stand to be more empathetic, daughter. You know better than anyone how difficult a time this is for someone in their position."

Emilia paused on the veranda, staring after her father. Slowly, she turned to stare up into the dusky sky. Her heart was heavy with sadness but for the first time since she could remember, the woe she felt was not for herself but for the small girl missing her mother and the man who could not take her pain away.

II

The following morning, Emilia dressed and fed her sisters before delivering them to their school. Their morning chatter was often the highlight of Emilia's day but that dawn, she could not get the sight of Amity Bawell's anguished blue eyes out of her head as if they were etched into her skull. Oh how she understood the poor child's misery and she desperately wished that there was a way to help the girl overcome her fresh loss. Of course, she knew from personal experience that there was no such way. The Bishop would tell her that time, family and community would help expel the pain but Emilia knew that was a lie he would tell everyone. Over and above that, Emilia found her mind traveling to Aaron's Bawell. He was still such a young man to be widowed. Abel had informed her that they had been wed eight years when cancer claimed Aaron's wife, Beth. She had been sickly for a very long while before finally succumbing to her grave. Amity had watched her mother wither away before her eyes and when she finally did go to her final rest, Aaron had immediately acted, taking Amity away from the horrible memories and the house in which her mother had suffered so greatly.

"No child should ever have to see their parent in a state like that," Able had said sadly. "Especially one so young. They cannot begin to reconcile what is happening. In a way, it is a blessing that your mother was take so quickly. She was never in agony which you girls had to witness."

Emilia swallowed the lump in her throat and nodded but she wasn't sure if she agreed. *Maybe mama wasn't in agony but we were. And some of us still are.* Emilia forced herself to think about Aaron and Amity. She vowed that she would befriend the newcomers at once. It would not make their life more bearable but it would help shoulder the burden they were carrying. The Bishop had been right about one thing; community and family did assist the process somewhat.

After sending the children off and promising to pick them up that afternoon, Emilia carefully constructed a basket of wicker and filled it with several thought-filled items. There was a freshly knit blanket she had intended to sell at the market, jars of preserves and honey, a mutton pie and a bouquet of wildflowers. She gently wrapped the basket in another wool blanket and carried the package outside and down the laneway. There was a charged nervousness about her as she knocked on the door to the Bawell house. There was no sign of movement from within the walls but the curtains were drawn. Emilia knocked again but to her disappointment, there was no response. *Ah, well I imagine Amity is in school and Aaron is off at work although Lord knows they should be home in their grief. I will just leave this here. I did not pen a note. Maybe I will run home, write a note and bring it back.* Emilia set the gift down on the small porch and was on her way to retrieve a pen and paper. Suddenly, one of the straps to her bonnet came loose and just before a short wind carried it off, Emilia reached up and snatched it back, her whole body turning. Lowering herself from the balls of her feet, she realized she was facing the Bawell house again. Aaron Bawell was standing at the door, staring at her strangely. He was wearing only a white cotton undershirt and a pair of trousers, his beard unkempt and his feet were bare. Even so, he looked incredibly handsome, his black hair a disheveled mess about his finely lined face. He looked down at the basket on the porch and then back to Emilia. She offered him a timid smile.

"My family sent you some goods to help you along," she called out. Again, his steely blue eyes looked at the package. Without a word, he turned and slammed the door behind him, leaving the present on the dusty deck.

"You must not be offended, daughter. He is grieving," Abel told Emilia when she reiterated what happened.

"I know he is grieving, father but even you have to admit that it was unfathomably rude!" Abel shrugged nonchalantly and took a sip of his tea.

"You must not forsake them in their time of need, Emilia. People often are the most trying during their darkest hour of need. It is God's way of testing you to see if you are capable of maintain humility and patience. Also, Aaron has agreed to come here for supper tomorrow evening." Emilia dropped her parring knife and stared at her father in disbelief.

"Oh father, you must stop beating a dead horse! You cannot believe that a recently widowed man is someone whom is interested in marrying your spinster daughter." Abel looked up sharply at her.

"Firstly, you are not a spinster. Not for the time being, mind you...and secondly, it is not my intention to push marriage upon a devastated man. I am merely suggesting you provide comfort to a man and a child who desperately require a support system. Everything is not sordid and dark, Emilia. You must learn that every cloud had a silver lining. And when you learn that, perhaps you can pass that information along to the Bawells." Contritely, Emilia looked at her hands and then continued peeling potatoes. Secretly she was pleased that Aaron and Amity were coming. She had been unable to stop thinking about the man, despite his brusque nature. *He is a hard man to reach, perhaps due to the circumstances.*

"Yes, father," she replied. "What shall I make for supper tomorrow night?"

"Well apparently anything but mutton," Abel jested lightly.

When Aaron and Amity appeared on the veranda of the Troyer home, something seemed different. Amity was no long sulky and angry. She was very quiet and seemed almost out of touch with what was occurring in her presence. Abel introduced her to Evelyn and Collette but she was as disinterested in the girls as Aaron was in Emilia. The entire grouping was a fiasco and Emilia wanted to escape. As the men and children sipped on lemonade on the porch, Emilia put the finishing touches on supper before calling everyone inside. The men seated at both ends of the table, grace was said and Emilia began to serve generous portions of fried beef cutlets, roasted potatoes and corn. Collette passed bread around the table.

"This is excellent, Emilia. You are a wonderful cook," Abel declared, taking a bite of his meal. She smiled at his transparency and he winked subtly in her direction.

"Thank you, father," she replied. She looked expectantly at Aaron but he continued to eat his food, unspeaking. Emilia felt her heart sink. She was expecting too much from this man. She did not know why she felt so drawn to him, why it was so important that he like her but she could not think of anything she wanted more than for him to look at her and say one kind word. Emilia sighed and put her fork onto her plate, her appetite suddenly depleted. She waited for the others to finish their meal before rising to clear away the dishes. Collette and Evelyn rose to help. When the three siblings were in the kitchen, Collette rolled her dark eyes heavenward.

"What a bore!" she exclaimed.

"Shhh!" Emilia hissed at her sister. "Lower your voice immediately!"

"That girl is odd," Evelyn piped up. "She doesn't say anything!"

Emilia turned and glared at her nine-year-old sister.

"Many people would say you are odd because you say too much! Shame on you both! They are guests in our home and we treat them with the respect they deserve. What's more is you do not ever judge a someone for you do not know where they have come from!" Evelyn looked aghast, completely unaccustomed to being reprimanded by Emilia. Her own limpid eyes filled with tears.

"I didn't mean harm" she whispered. "I'm sorry, Emmy. I respect our guests!"

Emilia was filled with remorse as she watched her sister's face but she stood firm.

"When you respect people, you do not speak ill of them behind their backs. I want you to carefully consider your words before you speak from this day forward. You can cause someone a great deal of harm with your language and imagine how ashamed you will feel if that person needed a friend but instead were only met with idle name calling. You two are better than that! You were raised to be charitable and kind. Do not disappoint papa and I." Nodding, both girls shuffled upstairs to avoid any further punishment. As they disappeared, Abel walked into the kitchen.

"You will make a good mother," he told her quietly.

"Did you hear those two?" Emilia asked, placing a dish towel onto the counter, shaking her head in disbelief, purposely ignoring her father's comment. Abel nodded.

"Yes, I heard them. And I heard what you told them."

"Well it's true. They were raised better than that," Emilia said, reaching into the ice box for the cobbler she had made for dessert.

"I heard something else also," Abel said, drawing closer. Emilia glanced up.

"What else did you hear, father?" Abel gently touched her face so she was looking at him. He smiled genuinely, his eyes twinkling with happiness.

"I heard you call me 'papa.'"

Emilia had just finished hanging the wash on the line when she heard a faint knock at the door. Hurriedly, she picked up the basket and rushed inside. Unceremoniously, she threw open the door and her breath caught in her throat.

"Mr. Bawell!" He had been staring blankly into the yard and seemed to snap out of his reverie when Emilia spoke his name.

"Emilia," he nodded. He had a faraway look in his eye and he bit his lip as if in concentration.

"Are you all right?" Emilia questioned, trying to make sense of why he was standing on the doorstep. Unconsciously, her hand swept through her hair, smoothly the flyaway strands.

"No." Emilia stared expectantly at him, waiting for an elaboration which did not materialize. She sighed. He was still determined to be standoffish and she had far too much to do that day than vie for his affection.

"Mr. Bawell, my father is at the shop if you would like to speak with him," Emilia offered. Aaron blinked at her as if he did not comprehend her words.

"No," he said again, in a flat, monotonous way. "I need you."

Emilia's heart fluttered and she shushed it in her head but a smile could not help but find its way to her lips.

"Oh?" she asked with some uncharacteristic coyness. Her smile faded with his very next words.

"My daughter has vanished. I need you to help me find her."

III

Night had fallen and there was still no trace of young Amity. Aaron Bawell sat perfectly still on a straight back chair, as if his soul had floated away from his body. A search party had formed and they had covered all of the hills and valleys in the district but no one had found a sign of the girl.

"She will turn up. She probably just got lost. They will find her," Abel told Aaron soothingly, trying to force his neighbor to eat and drink but Aaron was unhearing, unseeing and seemingly uncaring. The members of the community gathered in the bishop's home, waiting for word and speculating among themselves.

"Who would abduct a small Amish girl?" they wondered. "Our way is peaceful. This is unheard of!"

"She was not abducted," Emilia suddenly said, an epiphany hitting her full force. There was a murmur of skepticism as she began to pace excitedly, her mind racing.

"How can you know that, Emilia? This is commonplace with the English. Kidnapping and such. A stranger must have wandered off with her."

"No one wandered off with her," Emilia told them. "She has not been kidnapped."

"What do you believe happened to her?"

For the first time in hours, Aaron looked up, his once vacant eyes filled with hope.

"Where is my daughter, Emilia?" he begged, his voice hoarse with emotion.

"She went to where her mother is resting."

Amity had been walking for over seven hours, her little legs exhausted as she trekked toward her old district. It was Aaron himself who had found his small daughter, asleep on the side of the dirt road, completely hidden to eyes not searching. Her cheeks were caked in salted tears, her nose completely blocked from the endless crying her journey had seen. Aaron had flown off the carriage before it had come to a complete halt. He scooped up his daughter in strong arms and held her tightly but even that gesture did not wake the child from the depth of her sleep. Swaddling her like an infant, Aaron carefully placed her in the back of the wagon and sat with her as Abel took the reins and began the journey back to Latham District. Emilia sat in the wagon with father and daughter. Assured that Amity was still asleep, Aaron turned to the lovely blonde across from him. She could not make out his face as the wagon was dark and the night, moonless.

"How did you know?" he finally asked her. "How did you know where she had gone?"

Emilia was silent a moment. Ever since she had learned of Beth's death, it was as if a floodgate of memories had taken Emilia over. She began reliving every painful event which occurred from the moment her own mother had passed. When Aaron had arrived on the doorstep that afternoon, Emilia hadn't immediately made the connection but as time went on, it became clearer that Amity had not been taken and instead had run off somewhere. There was only one place the child wanted to be; with her mother. Of course Emilia knew that. That feeling was still very fresh in her own heart.

"I was Amity not too many years ago," Emilia told Aaron. "I understand how she feels."

There was a deep quiet from the other side of the transportation.

"I tried very hard," Aaron finally said.

"It is not easy," Emilia agreed.

"No. It is worse than that. Beth was sick for a great while. I had expected her to pass from when Amity was two years old. But she was a fighter, our Beth. She would get well and then get sick again, well and sick once more, each time getting worse and worse. Her body was failing. Everyone could see it including Beth. Our entire community knew it was only a matter of time. But Amity was just a baby. She only saw her mother. And she had so much hope that her mother would get well." Again, there was silence. Emilia opened her mouth to speak some words of comfort when Aaron took a breath.

"I despised my wife at the end of her life, Emilia. God help me, it's the truth. I loathed the fact that she would not give up and would continue to put our daughter through the trauma of watching her fall ill time and again. I am a despicable person. What kind of man wants his wife to die?" There was a catch in his voice and Emilia swallowed the lump in her own throat.

"The kind of man who cannot bear to watch others suffer," she answered quietly. "A very noble man. A man who loves his daughter so much that it tore him apart to watch her cry day after day for her mama." *A man like my father,* Emilia thought, her heart swelling with love for the man in the front of the carriage.

"I have been very uncouth to you, Emilia," Aaron suddenly said from the darkness. His voice was gruff.

"You have been grieving," she replied. "I do not consider a grieving man uncouth."

"No. That is not why I have been so uncivilized to you."

Emilia opened her mouth to protest but instead decided to wait for him to continue.

"When Beth found out she was dying, she made me promise to get married immediately so Amity would have a mother. She made numerous suggestions as to who should replace her. I agreed to placate her during her last days but the thought of marrying anyone else, of Amity calling anyone else 'mama' was horrifying and wrong. Some women in my community were overtly suggestive even prior to Beth's passing and when she finally did pass, there were knocks on my door quite literally the next day. That is why I made such a hasty decision to take Amity and leave."

"Ah, you thought I was one of the women vying for position of your wife," Emilia said slowly feeling her face blush crimson. *Oh papa! Do you see what your meddling has done now?*

"No, that's not what I believed, Emilia. I had seen you at church and you were so lovely, my breath actually halted when I laid eyes upon you. I had never felt that way about anyone. You are so beautiful but in a modest, unassuming form. I saw how well everyone has taken to you, how hard you work and how your sisters adore you. You are everything a man could hope for. I knew I had to stay far away from you. Yet when your father approached me in a neighborly fashion, I could not resist inviting you to supper. I wanted you near but I wanted you far away. Do you understand?"

Emilia almost laughed out loud.

"I understand exactly what you mean," she replied. "And now?"

Out of the dark, a large, calloused hand found hers. An unexpected shiver went up her spine at the touch. She squeezed his palm gently.

"And now the thought of marrying anyone other than you is horrifying and wrong." Aaron squeezed her hand back and for the first time since her mother died, Emilia felt the weight of the world lift off her shoulders.

She was actually happy.

END

The Wedding Dress

Chapter 1

Gabriela stared at her bank account, willing it to change. There was no way she was down to a hundred and twenty dollars. She wasn't getting paid for another three days! Even when she did get paid, a majority of it would get eaten up by her rent and groceries for that week. "Oh no," Gabriela said, laying her head on her arms. She didn't want to think about it, or look at it, or have anything to do with it. Unfortunately, when the problems are in your own life, you cannot exactly run away from them.

Gabriela wanted to call Bryan and get his support. She knew he would have all the verbal support she could want, but he wouldn't be able to loan her any money. His financial situation was just as bad as hers and he made even less money than she did. Once again, Gabby re-evaluated the idea of moving in with Bryan already. It would save them a few hundred bucks a month, and it wasn't so bad. After all, everyone was doing it.

"Maybe then, I would actually have money for a wedding dress," Gabby muttered to herself.

"Having a conversation with yourself again?" Reese asked her.

Gabby quickly minimized her bank account window. "Yes," she replied, trying to put aside her doubts to talk to her sister.

"You're starting to worry me. Turn that frown upside down!" Reese said, coming over and hugging Gabby.

Gabby couldn't help shaking her head and allowing a small smile to form on her lips. "Thanks, Reese." Reese started playing with Gabby's hair, brushing her fingers through its strands. Gabby closed her eyes and sunk into the sensation. It felt so calming to have her sister play with her hair as she had done since she was a little girl.

"Your graduation is in two weeks, isn't it?" Gabby asked, making slow conversation. Reese's hands felt so good.

"Yup! I can't believe I'm actually going to be done with high school. Then, I'm going to college, and that scholarship is seriously a blessing, don't you think?"

Gabby did her best at a nod. "Yes, I don't know how we would do it without that scholarship."

"Do you think Mom and Dad will come to my graduation?" Reese asked in a quiet voice. Gabby was glad she didn't have to look her sister full in the face as she answered.

"I don't know, Reese. Dad might not come because he thinks Mom will be there. Besides, he hasn't really been here for a while. I don't know. Mom might come."

"Do you think she'll bring her terrible boyfriend?"

"I don't know, Reese, but I want you to focus on your success, not on other people. You and only you have been the one responsible for getting yourself through high school. You have studied hard, and this is your time for a reward. I was thinking just you and me could go get ice cream at Scream

Cream, maybe not that night but maybe the next if you are too busy partying."

Reese knew that Gabby's money situation was tight, but she just didn't know how tight. Gabby didn't dare let Reese in on the secret. They just needed to get through the summer then Reese would be in college, and Gabby would somehow pull together enough money for just a small wedding.

"When are you going to go dress shopping?" Reese asked after a few moments of silence.

"I don't know, Reese. I will be going soon. Don't worry. You will be invited."

"Yay! You know I am so excited for you! I'll still be able to come home for Thanksgiving or fall break to wherever you guys are, right?"

"Of course, Reese!" Gabby said, finally turning and looking her sister in the eye. "Come here." Even though Reese was eighteen, Gabby was still her big sister at twenty-five. "You will always be my baby," Gabby said, trying to make Reese sit on her lap.

"No!" Reese wailed. "I shall not! I am too old to be sitting on anyone's lap."

"Mmhmm," Gabby smiled mischievously. "I'll just tell that to your striking college boyfriend when you get him."

"Eww!" Reese said. "I'm not going to sit on anyone's lap."

Gabby laughed. "Sure, you say that now. Shall I videotape you saying it and show to you in five years? Come on, help me finish making that garlic bread."

Two days later, Gabby decided to pay a visit to Bryan. They wanted to have their wedding in the middle of August. At this point, they hadn't done anything more than decide it would be held on Bryan's family farm. That decision was based on the fact that it would be a free venue, including free flowers.

"Hey, Baby," Bryan said when Gabby dropped by at dinnertime. "I made something healthy for once. You should be proud of me."

Gabby laughed. "Of course, I'm proud of you. Reese and I rebelliously did not make a salad with our meal last night, so you are doing better than me."

"Come here," Bryan said, pulling her close. He gave her a sweet kiss. When he pulled back, Gabby smiled. This was why she was with him. He always made her feel at home. "Go ahead and sit down. I'll get you a drink in a minute," Bryan commanded.

Gabby took a seat and watched Bryan careen around the kitchen, pouring drinks, draining whole wheat pasta, and preparing their plates. When they finally sat down, Gabby took his hand and listened to Bryan pray. "Thank you, God, for this meal you have given us the resources to have. Please keep giving us all that we need. Amen."

The two began eating, and Gabby finally got up the nerve to bring up the old wedding topic. "Do you think we will even be ready to get married in August? That's only two and a half months away. I'm just worried that we won't have everything ready."

Bryan sighed, but Gabby knew that his frustration was not aimed at her. "I know it's stressful. But, we've almost gotten the rings paid for." Gabby realized at that moment that she forgotten to bring her ring payment that evening.

"Sorry!" Gabby interrupted. "I forgot my payment tonight. I'm getting paid tomorrow, though. I can just give you the money then, right?"

Bryan nodded. "That's fine. I know you're tight too. But, look, we'll have a beautiful meadow, rings, our pastor will come, and gorgeous wildflowers. Maybe we can ask guests to bring a dish. I know it's not conventional," Bryan said in response to Gabby's strange look. "But, maybe they will understand. Feeding so many people can be a few thousand dollars."

"I know," Gabby nodded. "And you paint a beautiful picture. I like the way it sounds. The problem is that. . .I really want to wear a special dress. I've always dreamed of a gorgeous white wedding dress, and I just don't know if I will be able to afford one. I don't want our wedding to just pass by like it's not anything special. I want to look beautiful for you." Gabby's voice cracked with emotion, and she looked down to avoid crying.

Bryan reached over and pat her hand. "I know that it is important to you. It's important to me that you have the wedding just how you want it. But I want you to know that whatever you choose to wear, I will love it." That was when Gabby realized that her yearning to wear such a beautiful gown might not be because she wanted Bryan to think she was beautiful. Maybe she just wanted to feel beautiful for once, not for anyone else but for herself.

Chapter 2

On Saturday, Gabby left Reese sleeping at home in bed to peruse the local flea market. She needed to get Reese a graduation present, but she also didn't have a lot of money to spend on something like that. She had no idea what she wanted to get her sister, but she knew that she liked to read. Perhaps, Gabby could find a few books at a reasonable price.

Gabby was looking at a table of books, holding a couple in her hands. The three books were only twelve dollars altogether, and Gabby thought they would be a great present for Reese right before her last free summer. Gabby looked up, and her eyes fell on a shining white dress hanging on a mannequin the next stall over. Gabby left the three books on the table and walked toward the dress as if in a trance.

Her hand reached up to stroke the fabric. Just as her fingers were going to touch the fabric, Gabby wondered if she should. She looked around to see if anyone was watching her. She saw a small, elderly woman with her eyes trained on her.

"Oh, sorry," Gabby said, stumbling into an apology. "I'm sorry. I didn't know if it was alright to touch, but it's so...pretty."

"Go ahead," the woman said in a raspy but friendly voice. "You may touch it." Her smile encouraged Gabby just the bit she needed to have the courage. She turned back to the dress and stroked it. It was soft, almost like silk. The beadwork was amazing, with little detail stitched along the folds of the fabric. The bosom was covered with exquisite beadwork, and the waist came in before flowing out in a long skirt. The train was not overwhelming but still had a presence. It was as though someone had created a wedding gown out of Gabby's imagination.

Gabby's breath caught in her throat. She didn't want to turn away from the beauty. She stealthily scanned the dress for a price tag. Of course, there was not one. That must mean that the dress was handmade and would cost even more.

"Th-thank you," Gabby said, turning away from the dress and nodding to the woman. She took a backward step away from the dress and the woman.

"Are you getting married?" the woman asked, leaning forward encouragingly.

"Yes," Gabby nodded. "But, we don't have a date yet. It will still be a few months." Finally, she shrugged her shoulders and figured she might as well ask how much the dress cost. If she didn't, she would constantly wonder. At least with a number, she could walk away from it without feeling guilty. "How much is the dress?" Gabby nodded toward the wedding dress she had been studying.

The old woman smiled and leaned back. "Oh, that dress doesn't have a price. I'm sure you noticed. It is a beautiful and priceless piece. But," the woman continued speaking before Gabby could turn away. "I will let you wear the gown for free if you promise me one thing."

"What?" Gabby whispered, unable to wait to hear her words.

"You must live out your marriage according to God's will."

"I-uh-oh," Gabby seemed unwilling to respond. "I can wear it. . .for free?"

The woman nodded. "There's a veil that goes with the dress as well, but I must have you promise that your marriage will be uplifting to God. Can you do that?"

"I promise with my whole heart," Gabby said. She couldn't control the smile that spread across her face.

The woman nodded. "Very well. God, our good Lord, will hold you to your word. Now, just give me a moment to gather the dress and package it safely. Do you have a few minutes?"

"Yes, of course!" Gabby could hardly believe her good fortune. "Do you need any help? I could help you."

"That blue bag up there on the shelf, yes, that one. That's the veil. Go ahead and get that down, will you?" Gabby strained up to reach the high shelf, took down the bag, and could not help peering into the bag to examine the veil.

"What do you think?" the woman asked, nodding at the veil.

"It's amazing," Gabby said. The woman carefully took out the veil and used the comb part to place the veil on Gabby's head. She handed Gabby a small hand-mirror, and Gabby nearly cried. She looked like a real bride, not a bride who didn't have any money. Spontaneously, Gabby reached down and hugged the old woman. "Thank you," she sobbed out. The woman patted Gabby's back.

Finally, Gabby carefully folded the veil and put it back in the bag. She then helped the woman take the dress off the mannequin and store it in a garment bag.

"I have one more thing for you," the woman said as Gabby prepared to leave.The woman pulled out a thick book. "I want you to take a look at this. This dress, you see, has a long history. It has made many brides happy on their wedding day, and they all needed it in one way or another. I encourage you to find out about their stories and write your own as well."

Gabby took the thick, leather bound book in the crook of her arm and tried to give the woman one last hug while balancing her packages. "How will I find you again?" Gabby asked.

"I'm always right here," the woman assured her. "Come back after your wedding, and I'll be waiting."

Gabby smiled, thanked the woman one more time, then hurried out of the flea market, forgetting all about Reese's graduation present. The smile could not be wiped off her face. She carefully laid the dress across her backseat and could not help but sing along with every song on the radio. The only thing left to do was try it on. When she reached home, she carried the dress inside and explained the whole story to Reese who at first felt deceived that her sister had gone wedding dress shopping without her.

"I'm going to try it on," Gabby said. "Wait until I'm in it, okay? Don't come in!" Gabby shut the door with her sister outside and changed as carefully as she could into the wedding dress. Gabby could tell the dress had had sleeves at some point. But, it was now a sleeveless dress. The hem was a little long, but Gabby knew she could fix that. Around her waist, the dress fit perfectly. Gabby tucked the veil into place then opened the door with a smile.

"Sis!" Reese said. The smile filling her face was all that Gabby needed to see. "It's perfect isn't it?"

"Yes, it is!" Reese gave Gabby a hug. "I can't believe you are actually getting married!"

"It seems real now."

"It is real," Reese said. "I know Bryan would love you in this dress. I wish he could see it now."

"I know!" Gabby laughed. "But it has to be our secret. "No words to him about it. None, do you hear me?"

Later that night, Bryan came over. He got along well with Reese, and Gabby loved that about him. After all, she might not be Reese's official guardian, but she was Reese's home ever since their parents had started their incessant bickering.

The three were playing a game of Phase 10, and Reese kept smiling randomly at Gabby. "Is something wrong with you?" Bryan asked her. "Or do you two have a cheat going on?"

Both Gabby and Reese laughed. "Nope, we're not cheating," they said in unison.

"Okay, because that denial was totally believable. Come on, I know something is up." Gabby looked at Reese. They both shrugged, but Gabby could not longer keep the news in.

"I got my wedding dress today," Gabby said.

"What?! That's amazing, Gabby. Where is it? Can I see it? Was it expensive?"

"To all of those questions, the answer is no. Besides, the groom is never supposed to see the dress before the wedding day."

"I've got an idea," Bryan said, leaning forward. "Want to get married tomorrow?"

"Sorry," Gabby shook her head. "Pastor is occupied tomorrow. Besides, I'm not ready yet."

"Aw," Bryan visibly drooped. "I guess we should probably wait until we have rings, huh?"

"That would be important!" Gabby said. She gave Bryan a playful kiss and was glad that she did not feel as desperate for a dress as she had that morning.

Chapter 3

Gabby carefully opened the book the woman had given her the day before. In the excitement of trying on the dress and spending time with Bryan, she hadn't thought about it again until she and her sister were leaving church. She hadn't told her sister about the book or how exactly she had gotten the dress, but she had told her enough to be satisfied.

The book appeared to be some sort of journal. On the pages were handwritten notes, some in cursive, some printed, and clearly not all done by the same person. Beside each handwritten note was a picture of a woman wearing the wedding dress. Gabby ran her hands over the first picture. The dress had had sleeves, just as Gabby suspected. The picture looked old, and it was worn around the edges. But it had stayed faithfully in the book. Beside it was a note.

"Teresa Daniels, age twenty-four. Married to Bertram Frantz, age twenty-four, on May 7, 1978. My parents had both died when I was five. I had been living with a family friend since then. The boy I grew up living next to asked me to marry him, but I didn't have any money for a wedding, let alone a beautiful dress. I met this wonderful young woman who loaned me a dress that she had just finished making. She told me to tell my story and live my marriage in a way that would make God pleased with me. I am determined to do just that. My adoptive parents may not have enough money to pay for a wedding, but this wedding dress shows just how much God is looking out for us."

Underneath the note was Teresa Frantz's contact information. In different handwriting was a little note that said she had died in a car accident in 2004. Gabby suddenly felt as though she was holding something very sacred. The dress was only used perhaps once a year, if that, and Gabby hungrily read through each story. Each woman had something to say about how she did not have enough money or something had befallen her. Gabby wondered why their contact information was there. Did they really want someone to talk to them? And what did they want to talk about?

Gabby pictured herself eight years from now with a few small children. She would always remember how she had gotten her wedding dress. What would she say to someone else who was going to use it? Gabby could only smile.

She selected two of the most recent weddings and decided to write to their email addresses. Her message was simple.

"Hi, my name is Gabriela. I'm going to use the wedding dress. I found your information in the book, and I was wondering if you'd like to meet and have a coffee."

Gabriela went to bed at close to two in the morning. "I am so not going to be awake for work in the morning," Gabby said. She had received her payment in her account over the weekend, and Gabby spent a little time that Monday morning paying her bills. It was just as nasty as ever. Even though she had a wedding dress now, she still would not be able to save any money after paying everything necessary. She sighed and shook her head. "It's okay," she told herself.

The workday passed well enough, but Reese was celebrating when she got home because she only had two more exams before she was officially done with school. Gabby spent some of the evening quizzing Reese before she gave herself the luxury of checking her email. She had received a reply.

"It's nice to hear from you, Gabriela. I would love to meet for coffee. How does Wednesday at lunch hour sound? Would it be possible for me to meet you at the Starbucks in Clayton?

Annabel"

Gabriela rejoiced over the email. She couldn't wait to meet this woman and unravel a bit more of the dress mystery.

When it finally came time for her Wednesday lunch hour, Gabby drove as quickly as she could to the Starbucks. She ordered and looked around for Annabel. She finally found her, and the two shook hands in a formal manner.

"I'm so glad you reached out and contacted me," Annabel said. "I wondered if anyone ever would."

Gabby smiled excitedly. "I can't believe the dress was first loaned out in 1978. It still looks so new."

"Well," Annabel surmised. "The sleeves were taken off, and I think some extra beadwork was added."

"Still," Gabby smiled. "It's like I'm wearing a little bit of history."

Annabel laughed. "Yeah, it's magical the way that woman wants to help us. It's like she can just sense the desperation in someone."

"So, what's your story?" Gabby asked, wanting to fill in the blanks Annabel's note had left.

Annabel nodded. "I was eighteen when I got the wedding dress. I know, I was young. I didn't want to get married yet, but my boyfriend had gotten me pregnant. I had just found out a few days before. I had talked to my boyfriend, and he and I decided we would just have a quiet wedding, a justice of the peace deal. I didn't want to do that, but I knew we needed to do something quickly. I didn't want to be one of those boldly pregnant brides. But I was so frustrated with the whole situation, that I had just decided I would wear an old dress. It didn't matter.

"When I saw that wedding dress, though, I couldn't help but be drawn to it. When the woman told me it was free for my use as long as I lived a godly marriage, I couldn't believe my good fortune. We had a justice of the peace wedding, but I was wearing a gorgeously beautiful wedding gown. I will never forget that woman's generosity." Annabel shook her head.

"So, it made your day magical?" Gabriela asked in excitement.

Annabel laughed aloud. "Yes, it sure did. My wedding may not have been what I had imagined it to be when I was fifteen or sixteen, but it was much better than it would have been under the circumstances. Now, I have Gracen, and she's getting close to her second birthday."

"Wow! That's so amazing."

"What's your story?" Annabel leaned forward and listened as Gabriela told her about her all the financial troubles she had had. Gabriela and Annabel continued chatting until the last possible minute.

"I really need to get back to my job," Gabby said, "Or I could lose it. That is definitely not what I need right now. Look, I really enjoyed talking to you. Maybe we could get together again, and I could meet Gracen?"

"I'd like that," Annabel said. "I'll talk to you later."

Chapter 4

Gabriela finally got a reply from the other woman she had contacted about meeting: Brianne. Brianne's story had seemed really tragic, and Gabriela couldn't wait to hear about it from the woman's lips.

After the introductions, Gabriela leaned forward for Brianne's story. "I'm really glad you wanted to talk," Brianne said. "I feel like this dress has created a secret group."

"Have you ever talked to Annabel?" Gabriela asked.

"Annabel. . .Annabel. I don't think so. Was she married after me?"

"I don't remember," Gabriela said. "But I have her number. Maybe we could all three get together or even more brides."

Brianne smiled. "I like the idea. I am definitely willing to contribute. Okay, so here's what happened to me. My problem was not so much a financial one as I read in so many stories. Instead, my problem was a big fire. About five days before the date our wedding was set, some sort of electrical malfunction sparked in our house. My family lost everything. Insurance took care of the problem financially, but the dress I had so carefully picked out months before along with my shoes and veil had been consumed by the fire. Trying to get a dress five days before a wedding is pretty much impossible.

"But, this beautiful old lady performed a miracle. She let me borrow the dress. It was much better than the dress

I had originally picked. Better than that, it was ready for the wedding two days early." Brianne shook her head. "I had thought I might need to call off the wedding. I was freaking out. I couldn't even go to work I was so stressed out. I had a few burn marks from escaping the house, but the dress covered them nicely. They can't even be seen in the photos."

"Wow!" Gabby said, soaking in her new friend's story. "Wow." She was silent for a few minutes as Brianne's story sunk in. "Did you know that there have been thirty-three weddings in that dress? I'll be number thirty-four."

"When is your wedding?" Brianne asked.

"It'll be mid-August, right after my sister moves into her college dorm. She's been living with me."

"Would you mind if I rudely invited myself to your wedding?" Brianne smiled.

Gabby laughed. "Of course not. You are welcome. It's going to be a small wedding, and we ask that each guest bring a dish of food, a sort of potluck. We really don't have the money for much more, but I would be honored for you to come."

After meeting the two brides, Gabby wanted to meet more. She kept setting up even more appointments with brides. She had one last meeting planned before her wedding. This meeting took a few weeks to set up. By the time Gabby met her, it was the first day of August.

"What's your story?" Gabby asked impatiently. The question had become one of which she could not wait to ask each new woman. Hallie had been married almost ten years ago.

"My story's probably a bit different from some others," Hallie shook her head. Gabby had agreed to come to her house because Hallie had three young children. Hallie wanted them to be able to play and stay out of their hair while the two women talked. "I was poor. I couldn't buy a wedding dress. That much is as normal as for any of us women."

Gabby nodded, anticipating more.

"My story becomes interesting after I married Mark. Did the lady have you make a promise?"

Gabby nodded. "Yes, I promised that I would live my marriage according to God's will."

Hallie accepted Gabby's words. "Yes, I promised the same thing. At the time, I promised it because it seemed such an easy exchange for the dress. But it wasn't as easy as I thought it would be. The first year of marriage was so difficult. I looked back on the innocence I sported on my wedding day, and I would shake my head. How had I thought I loved Mark?" Hallie was quiet as she remembered. "I was sure that we were going to get a divorce. You see, his family lives on the other side of the country. I know he was really close to them, but he agreed that living here would be the best solution for us.

"But, it was like he had forgotten that. We argued almost every night. I started to hate him. He made me cry so much." Hallie shook her head, and Gabby should see the tears brimming in her eyes. "I started fantasizing about running away and going a place where he wouldn't find me. Then, I remembered my promise. I tried to weasel my way out of it, saying that the fighting was Mark's fault. I blamed him, but I knew I needed to take credit for my part. So, I started serving Mark instead of myself.

"Even when I was tired, I would make dinner. I would clean up without complaint. He noticed after a month, and I felt him become more tender toward me. We were finally able to talk through what had been happening. That was the best day of my life, the day that we finally talked it all through without screaming. I finally slept next to him and felt connected to him again.

"Gabby, that promise is going to be hard to keep. You will probably get angry with your fiance sometimes, but don't walk away. The weak walk away; it's the strong that keep fighting."

Gabby hugged Hallie as a few tears spilled over. "Thank you, Hallie. I needed to hear those words. They were just what I needed." Before Gabby left Hallie's house, she invited her to her wedding. "I know it is only two weeks, but if you think you can come, I would really like it. Don't be shy about bringing your husband and children."

Chapter 5

On the day of her wedding, Gabby carefully donned the dress. It was to be a simple ceremony. Only her sister would stand beside her. Bryan was having his best friend stand beside him. At that moment nothing felt simple about Gabby as she waited for Reese to calmly do up the back.

"I can't believe it's really the day," Gabby said.

Reese smiled. "Yeah, I'm pretty sure I'm having the most exciting first weekend home from college out of all of my friends." Of course, her statement made Gabby start asking about all of Reese's new friends. She had to make sure that her baby sister was doing well and having fun in college.

"Is it done?" Gabby asked.

Reese nodded. "It's done. You're all ready."

"Well, not completely," Gabby said. "I look fine, but I feel a bit nervous about walking down that aisle."

"Why?" Reese asked. "Are you unsure about Bryan?"

"No," Gabby shook her head. "I know he is perfect for me, well, as perfect a fit as someone can be with my rather strange personality."

Reese laughed. "Then, what is making you nervous?"

"I guess it just hit me that this is a lifelong commitment. I love Bryan, and I just don't want anything to go wrong. What if we start living together, and he does annoying things that get on my nerves?"

"Like what?"

"Like leave his socks on the bed."

"Then tell him to take his socks off," Reese shrugged. "It's not that hard. Look, if you love him and you know that for sure, then you just have to go through the bad stuff and remember that. Then you'll get to the good times, and it'll be all worth it."

"Alright, my sister the wise," Gabby smiled. "What time is it?"

Reese looked at her phone. "We still have thirty minutes."

"What a long thirty minutes that'll be!" Gabby sighed, carefully sitting in her dress.

Reese laughed aloud. "I thought you just said you were nervous to do it, and now you can't wait to go down the aisle."

Gabriela laughed with her sister. "When you get to this point, I will be right by your side and remind you of everything you just said. Meanwhile, you'll just be like. No, I'm nervous! Let me be nervous by myself!"

Gabriela's friend Erica burst into the bedroom just then. "Hey! Wow, Gabby! You look so amazing!" Erica was the unofficial photographer. She had a professional camera and had done some photo shoots. A free photographer was her wedding gift to her friend. "Look, we don't have a lot of time, but I wanted to get a few pictures of just you in all your bridal beauty, then maybe a few with Reese. Hey, Reese! How are you?" Erica said in one breath.

Gabby laughed. "Oh, Erica, I knew there was a good reason we were friends." Erica took all the photos she wanted with Gabby sitting, standing, lounging, smiling, and serious.

"Alright, Reese, get in there with your sister." After a few more shots, Erica hovered over to the door. "Alright, I believe we have five minutes before your little flower girl will start her march. Let's get you safely down these stairs."

Gabby carefully maneuvered the stairs with the help of her sister and friend. The stairs were not very wide and definitely not prepared to have brides tramping up and down them. She finally stood by the back doors.

"Ready?" Reese asked.

Because Gabby had decided against having their estranged father walking her down the aisle, Reese would be walking right beside her.

"I think so," Gabby answered. "But ask me again in a minute, and I might have a different answer."

"You've got this, Sis."

"Thanks."

Erica reappeared as the music started to assist the flower girl on her way. Next went the ringbearer. After that came Gabby and Reese. It was a simple, small wedding, just as Gabby had dreamed it. Best of all was Bryan's face when she came through the doors of the back of the farmhouse.

His smile was genuine and delighted, and Gabby looked only at him as Reese guided her steps down the aisle. When she reached the altar, she placed her hands in Bryan's, smiling into his eyes and wondering how she had ever doubted her decision to marry him.

"I love you," she whispered as the pastor was talking to them. He mouthed the words back and gave her hands a squeeze. Suddenly, the ceremony, including a candle lighting, a song sung by a friend, and a short talk from the pastor seemed all too long to Gabby. After what seemed an eternity, the words she had wanted to hear for so long pierced her thoughts.

"You may now kiss the bride."

Gabby kissed Bryan, leaning into his lips. When they pulled back, Gabby felt the magic of the moment lingering. "You're my husband," she whispered, incredulous.

"And you, my dear, are my wife." Bryan let go of one of her hands, facing the audience. The pastor announced them, and Bryan paused before they started down the aisle. "This is my wife!" he shouted, his pleasure clear as he lifted up their joined hands in victory. Gabby started laughing. Suddenly, a huge cheer rose up from the back of the rows of seats. Gabby looked over and counted five of the former brides that she had met.

"Yes, Gabriela!" They screamed together. While Gabby had not pictured her wedding as loud as a ballgame, she couldn't help laughing aloud.

Bryan carefully led her down the steps, and they entered the old farmhouse. As soon as they were inside, Bryan turned to her and kissed her passionately. "You are the most beautiful bride I have ever seen," he whispered. "And tonight, I will make you mine." Gabby trembled with anticipation, leaning in for another kiss.

A week later, Gabby carefully zipped the wedding dress into the garment bag for the last time. She took out the book and carefully glued in a photo of herself wearing the dress. She smiled at the photo then took up a pen and began writing in her best cursive beside the photo.

"Gabriela Winfox, age twenty-five. Married to Bryan Davis on August 21, 2016. This dress changed my life. Not only did it give me a chance to have the kind of wedding I would never have had on my budget, but it showed me the friendliness and generosity this kind of world doesn't see very often. It made me promise to be a more generous person and to look for opportunities to help others. I didn't have any money for a nice wedding, and my fiance and I feared we would not be able to throw a wedding. Determined to get married, because we knew it was right, I thought I would never have a wedding dress. I was wrong. Please, contact me. I would love to talk to you, and I know that the brides I met would love to talk to you as well. We are in this together."

Gabriela signed her name under her words and closed the book with a solemn thud. "Thank you, God," she said as she loaded the dress, veil, and book into the back of her car. She was on her way to the flea market.

HER AMISH ROMANCE
AMANDA ROBERS

Chapter 1: Just an Amish Girl

Naomi Zook never took pleasure in extravagant things. Her name Naomi, however, did literally mean, pleasant. Even when she became of age to experience Rumspringa, the time in which Amish girls and boys are allowed to experience the outside world, she did not find joy in living life outside of her quiet Amish community. She was a simple Amish girl through and through. She was also incredibly shy. Anyone who ever met or associated with Naomi would have few things to say about her, good, bad, or otherwise. She came from the Zook family; they lived a more or less traditional Amish-style life... no electricity, no cars, no cell phones. Her father was a woodworker and her mother was a quiltmaker. Naomi took on her mother's trade of quilt-making, in addition to making Amish-style dolls, and knitted slippers. Their family's lifestyle was certainly a humble way of life and nobody would dare say anything different. Even among the other Amish families in the community, no one had a bad thing to say about the Zooks.

Naomi, 18, spent her days split between assisting at the one-room schoolhouse, making quilts, sewing dolls, milking the family cow, and feeding the chickens. Naomi's family didn't own a whole farm like some families, but they had one cow for a milk and a dozen chickens for eggs. Naomi didn't love making quilts for her mother's business, but you would never know because not a single complaint ever escaped between her lips in front of the others. Naomi's mother, Rebekah Zook, was even more conservative that Naomi, and believed that Naomi existed simply to serve her. Naomi, being the only girl of six children, found herself doing a significant amount of the housework as well as sewing.

Being not only the only girl, but also the oldest, she was a very mature young lady, who wanted to not just sew her brother's torn clothes, but also, she desired to sew overalls for her future husband, whoever he was. She didn't find anything interesting about the "English boys," their cigarettes, their booze, or their addiction to their thumbs. She didn't understand what was so interesting about a bunch of colored candies in a row. What exactly was so fascinating on the phone that kept them from missing out on real life? None of them knew how to watch a sunset, to sit quietly without speaking or playing on their phones, or enjoy the tranquility of an evening fire.

She didn't understand why some of her girlfriends grew up and chose to leave the Amish community. She did understand, however, that some things, none of the girls liked, not even her. Being a woman in an Amish community, meant you needed to do almost everything. But in fact, Naomi didn't mind doing everything, but what she did want was a supportive husband by her side. Someone who would help her maintain a few animals, maintain some income for the house, and eat her cooking experiments in the kitchen.

Of the few things that she enjoyed from Rumspringa was some of the "modern" ingredients that she could use in baking and cooking. How easy it was to make a cake with premade icing (not that she didn't mind making her own icing.) How easy it was to buy a large tub of butter, rather than to make her own! Easy come easy go. Sometimes she worried about how she loved some of the conveniences of the outside world, but still, she was Amish through and through. Naomi even found a love of African pottery. She experienced the arts during her time away from the community, saw art museums, bought unique art supplies with her limited savings from selling Amish dolls, and even took an African pottery class.

Whenever Naomi expressed a desire for anything other than quilt-making, working hard for the family, feeding the chicken, milking the cow or cooking dinner, Naomi's mother would sigh with disgust. Although she didn't say anything, she didn't have to. One look from her mother and she would certainly not utter a word about wanting pottery supplies. For certain, her mother would remind her immediately that she chose to remain Amish. Her mother said almost every day with her face "Thank God that she will not bring shame to her family with interests in silly things such as African pottery and boxed cake mixes! Good Lord save us all."

Chapter 2: Traded Goods

One day, on Naomi's route to deliver quilts, dolls, slippers, and other sewn and knitted goods, she was surprised to find herself blushing at the door of the Kings' house when a young man called Amos answered the door. She had seen Amos at church meetings, barn-raisings, and the like, but she never had a conversation with him. She usually did not have a delivery from the King's home for any sewn goods, because their grandmother was, of course, also a homemaker, and used to make quilts herself. These days, however, their grandmother had been very sick in bed, due to a genetic disease called Cystic Fibrosis, that seemed to take over the poor woman's body. Although it was hardly uncommon for some diseases to crop up inside families, there was little the Kings' could do for their grandmother except to keep her comfortable.

They couldn't do much for her simply because of the nature of the disease; it certainly wasn't due to a lack of monetary resources, as they had a very nice-sized farm. The King's farm employed many children of families in the village who did not have their own farm. They were also always generous with what they had. Their names seemed to fit their finances, but they were among the humblest of families in the community. They were not only Kings on Earth, but they would be kings in Heaven too. Namoi was sure of that. Naomi's mother, Rebekah, never spoke about the King family but then again, she never spoke about any family other than her own.

When Amos opened the door to their home to accept the quilt a small toothy smile crossed his face. Naomi was surprised to see Amos smiling at her, as he had never paid her any attention before in the community. When she thought about it, she never really noticed him either, but here she was standing in front of his door. Amos begins speaking with her and asked her to come inside while he obtained payment for the quilt that his grandmother ordered. His grandmother used to be one of the best quiltmakers, but she wanted one from

Rebekah because she knew the quality of her work. Amos asked Naomi to come inside and have a glass of lemonade. It was not polite to leave the young lady standing on her doorstep after all. As Naomi came inside she immediately noticed that everything was in order. Everything had its place. Nothing was overdone or too exquisite. The only thing that revealed the Kings' families' wealth, besides the farm, of course, was the solitary grandfather clock that stood in the corner. Amos caught Naomi staring at the grandfather clock, and slightly embarrassed explained that it was a family heirloom. Amos didn't want Naomi to think that they were extravagant people. He knew that her family members were simply people, much like his.

Naomi was trying her hardest to listen to Amos' words about the grandfather clock but couldn't help but notice the beauty of his face. Everything from his black hat that every unmarried boy wore, to the sharp high edges of his cheekbones made her smile. He had slightly worn skin and calluses on his hands from working on the farm, but there was color in his cheeks and a bounce in his step. His hair was a light brown color, and his eyes were a precious dark brown. She found herself getting lost in his eyes and his high cheekbones and almost forgot that Amos was speaking. Amos paused and asked her if she didn't like her lemonade because she wasn't drinking it. She had almost forgotten entirely about her lemonade due to fact that she was gazing at Amos. Slightly embarrassed she drank her lemonade quickly. Amos offered another glass of homemade lemonade, and she shook her head saying she had to get back to her mother's house. Immediately. He then offered a silver of shoe-fly pie, but Naomi couldn't deny a well-made slice of shoe-fly pie. After all, who could turn down shoe-fly pie? Amos gave her payment in the form of more food than was necessary. He loaded her sack with cucumbers, tomatoes, fresh bread, home-made cheeses, a gallon of chicken corn soup, a bottle of home-made wine, and a jar of home-made peanut butter. Naomi tried to refuse at least the bottle of wine, but Amos insisted.

As she turned to go, he asked her to wait. Oh, Naomi, if you don't mind can you please make a few dolls for my young cousins. When you bring them, I'll certainly have a few more jars of home-made peanut butter ready for you. Amos' smile spread across his face like the stars lighting up the night sky on a clear night.

Chapter 3: How Could It Feel Like This?

A few days later, Naomi found herself bumping into Amos almost everywhere she went. How could it be that no matter where she was, Amos was there? After church on Sunday, Amos stayed for singing and was seated only a few seats away from her. She was wishing that he would ask to take her home or ask her out on a date, but nothing of the sort happened. After the singing, the youth were mixing, chatting, and talking as usual. Finally, Amos approached and made small talk. "How is your mother?" he asked Naomi. "Oh, fine, thank you, you know busy making quilts of course. She really truly loved your peanut butter, and she would never admit it, but she loved the wine too!" Naomi replied.

Amos laughed, and Naomi could almost feel his laugh reverberate through her soul. Naomi thought to herself that maybe she could even marry Amos. How could it be that without even touching his hand or passing more than a few minutes together she could feel like this? Amos' smile crept across his face because he wanted very much to ask Naomi to go out with him. He knew very well that Naomi had already turned down the opportunity to leave the Amish community, and so did he. He was not interested in what the outside world had to offer. Although he enjoyed some small pleasures of the outside world, he did not find that it was necessary to leave his family and his home just to have a simpler or easier life. It took him less than 24 hours to get used to the idea of flipping a switch and having electricity, lights, and a hot oven. Regardless of these conveniences, he never for a moment wanted to give up his Amish upbringing, family, values, and culture. Now he was even more certain of his decision as he saw something in Naomi that warmed his heart. What he would now, he just wasn't sure, but he would leave that thought process for another day.

The two found themselves with an awkward pause in the conversation as they realized that everyone had stopped speaking except for the two of them. Naomi suddenly bid him good night so as not to draw too much more attention to their conversation or time spent together. Naomi leaned in to give Amos an awkward half-hug that clearly wanted to be something more. She leaned in with one arm and pulled Amos into a tight hug that Amos returned half-heartedly. Actually, Amos wanted to give her a full-on frontal hug with both arms and kiss her forehead, but instead, he embraced her quickly and said good night.

Naomi quickly noticed that everyone was looking, and so she walked way in a hurried fashion. She met her mother outside the door of the church gathering. Immediately her mother had questions "Who was that boy you were hugging?" "The son of Faith King, no?" The questions and comments continued, "He's a good boy, you know, but you have no business starting anything with any boy. Naomi, you know very well that we need you here at the house. With all your brothers to feed and the house to clean, Naomi, you mustn't think about boys for a good long while..." her mother stated quite bluntly. That was it. Immediately the end of that conversation. "How was your friend, Ruth, darling?" asked Naomi's mother. "Oh, fine, yeah she's working on the farm, of course." "Like, a good Amish daughter, very, very good," replied Naomi's mother.

Chapter 4: The Usual Rhythm

A few weeks passed since Naomi had seen Amos. Rebekah had hoped that her daughter had forgotten entirely about this boy nonsense, but, in fact, quite the opposite was occurring for Naomi. The more time she stayed without seeing Amos, the more she daydreamed about marrying Amos, having her own family, having her first baby, making her own home, and maybe even making pottery too! Needless to say, she kept all those thoughts quiet to herself. After all, there were things that needed to be attended to at the house as usual.

Naomi continued her days, more or less, as usual. From 4 am to 6 am she was up bright and early, to tend the family cow and the few chickens. She fed the animals, collected any eggs, cleaned the trough, and refilled the water bowl for the chickens. Around 6 am she drank some warm milk and fried some doughnuts for everyone to eat for breakfast. The days passed like this in a very predictable pattern. After breakfast, there were house chores, cleaning the bathroom, washing the dishes, and inevitably, in the afternoon hours when it was simply too hot to be outside, Naomi sat wither mother in the parlor making quilts together. Plus, three days a week Naomi helped with teaching at the school.

There was only the sound of knitting needles clicking against each other, and the occasional comment from her mother about her progress on the quilts, until her brothers came home from school in the mid-afternoon hours. Naomi's mind stirred to one thing as it drew near the weekend. There was a barn-raising this weekend and she was bound to see Amos at the barn-raising. Everyone in the community always attended a barn-raising. It was coming to the end of the summer and fall was trying ever so hard to make its appearance. The leaves on the trees were still all green, but she could almost feel fall in the crisp fresh air of the countryside.

One of the things that she loved about her life was that the air was always fresh. In addition, fall was her favorite season. The air was also fresh with the smell of the animals sometimes, especially in the planting season, but she didn't mind that at all in comparison to the pollution, the cigarette smoke, and the nonsense that occurred in the city. Soon, the leaves would change colors, from greens to vibrant yellows, bright oranges, and raging reds. As a child, she loved to make leaf piles and jump in them. She always thought that she was just like every other child until she went on Rumspringa. Then she knew, she wasn't like all the other children. She actually liked her lifestyle better. Her life was not intruded upon by the outside culture of the others, their technology, and constant addiction to their phones. She could not accept how much the youth her own age were tip-tap-tapping away on their iPhones and i-whatevers.

Her mind wandered back to the upcoming barn-raising. The barn simply had to go up before the first frost. A newly married couple were starting their own small farm, and the community wanted to support the new family unit. She always loved barn-raisings. They naturally were a lot of work for everyone, and the women spent all day cooking, catering to the men, and bringing food and water to them, but she was always impressed by their ability to build a barn in one day. It's amazing what the whole community does when it comes together.

Chapter 5: Barn-Raising Day

Finally, the day of the barn-raising arrived. It was a beautiful early Saturday morning and the sun was not quite able to make an appearance yet when Amos got out of bed and donned his denim overalls and workmen's boots. Amos loved barn-raising days. He loved his family's farm too, but what he loved more was construction. Any task or project that allowed him to get his hands dirty literally, he loved, especially construction. Building something, feeling a part of something, feeling a part of a structure that would make his community stronger was more important than almost anything to him, except, God and his family. Recently though his mind seemed to wander to Naomi. She was a smart young lady, smart enough to understand the value of family and hard-work, and was, well, quite attractive too. After all, how could he not notice? Perhaps she liked him too? Did he like her? Her soft brown curls wrapped around her face, as soft as a peach from his mother's garden. He barely felt her cheeks graze his face when she went in to give him a hug at the church singing. He wasn't quite ready to admit that he had feelings for her, but after all, eventually, he wanted to marry a nice girl and start his own life. Amos pushed the thoughts of Naomi out of his head as he got ready to head to the location of the barn-raising with his father, mother, brothers, and sisters. Being one of 10 meant that there was always work to do, but it also always meant that there was an extra set of hands ready. Amos always loved being a part of a big family. He loved the feeling of being surrounded by those who love him in a home filled with laughter, singing, and even the smell of fresh bread and homemade wines. What more could you ask from life?

As Amos, his family, and the entire town gathered at the site of the barn-raising, Amos caught himself scanning the horizon for Naomi. How silly of me, he thought. Why am I looking for Naomi on the day of the barn-raising? The men and boys gathered, as the oldest and most experienced engineer in the community gave instructions and assigned tasks according to the skill level of each worker. Boys were to handle cutting and passing the plywood to the young men who assisted the leads of each group who were setting the foundation for the barn. The foundation was the hardest part. Once the foundation was finished there was no need to worry about the rest. The rest of the barn almost seemed to complete itself with the number of hands they had on deck.

Naomi found herself occupied through maintaining the food tables, arranging fruits, vegetables, cheeses, bread, and even hamburgers and hot dogs. On special days, they feasted even with "English food." Who didn't like a good hamburger, right? She kept her mind occupied with the festivities and enjoyed the fact that she was assigned to such a large task. Actually, it wasn't a very large task in comparison with building a barn, but still, she was always given more responsibilities than some of the other girls who never took a barn-raising seriously. They thought of it as a way to get escape responsibilities for the day and hide somewhere in the shade flirting with a boy who also found it more important to flirt than to prepare lumber.

As the day passed, the hungry team of workers assembled in the line, and orchestrated the food line. She had it down to a science. There was space for people to pass on both sides of the tables quickly, and as they filled their plates and stomachs, she refilled the baskets of food. Just as the basket of fresh rolls was looking empty, she looked up to find Amos reaching for a roll. He locked eyes with her, and startled said," Oh, hi Naomi, sorry, I didn't see you there." "Hi Amos, how are you doing today?" replied Naomi. "Great, thanks, you know, I love barn-raising days, then again, most of us do." Answered Amos. "Sure, of course," Naomi replied. Amos caught Naomi off-guard and said, "You look awfully nice today," "Oh, it's just the same thing I wear every day, but I am excited about seeing the new barn." replied Naomi.

The two laughed. "That must be it then," said Amos. Growing more self-conscious of the line going around them, Naomi suddenly remembered the basket of rolls. "Hey Naomi, are you going to refill the rolls or do I have to do it?" shouted Rebekah, Naomi's mother. "Mom, I was just..." and then Naomi was interrupted. "You were just, what?" asked her mother. "Nothing," said Naomi. When Naomi looked up Amos was gone. Certainly, he had to eat of course, but why did her mother look up at exactly the same time when she had finally spotted Amos?

Chapter 6: Trouble Lurking

Meanwhile in the corner of the room stood, Linda Stoltzfus, one of the busy bodies of the community. Everybody knew who the busybodies were, but nobody cared. Nobody took them seriously, but Linda on that day wanted to be taken seriously. Had she just seen Amos flirting with Naomi? Or was it Naomi flirting with Amos? No, that can't be. Naomi was such a plain boring girl, just doing whatever her mother asked or wanted. She was a few years younger than Naomi but she had her eye on Amos for quite some time. She certainly was not going to let some nose-wiping girl like Naomi snatch Amos out from her under her feet, now was she? Well, she would see about that. Amos, after all, was a catch. Almost every girl pined after Amos, his dark brown eyes, his rough, strong hands, and of course his family had a delightfully large farm and income. His family was well-to-due as far as standards in Amish communities went, and yet they were also well-respected. It would be a score for any young lady to marry Amos King. She would not let Naomi get in the way. Absolutely not!

She would have to be a bit coy about it, not to make people think badly of her, of course. She had her own reputation to think about too. She knew what everyone said about her, that she talked too much for her own good, but otherwise, was a nice young lady. Linda watched Amos and Naomi's small interactions through the day. She watched as Naomi specifically approached Amos near the construction zone and offered him a tall glass of water. She even caught a wide toothy smile spread across his face. That couldn't be, could it? That's when she knew what she had to do. The only thing to do was to keep Amos away from Naomi and to make Amos think that she was involved with another boy already. That Roy Miller. Why not? Roy Miller was just one year older than Naomi, and he had a crush on her for years, but she either never noticed or simply wasn't interested. If she started telling the others that Naomi and Roy were going out, Roy could jump on the opportunity to actually ask her out. That would ruin any chance of Amos and Amos becoming an "item."

As the barn was going up and the day was closing, Linda found herself a quiet corner with some of the older women in the community who lived for gossip. Some of these women barely had anything to do all day, so they discussed the potential matches for their grandchildren, their neighbor's children, and basically anyone of the age to marry. Linda found her opportunity and went for it. "You know," started Linda "Naomi and Roy are getting awfully close to each other. Have you seen the way Roy looks at Naomi? Now I know that Naomi's mother really needs the female help at home, but it's time that she is allowed to have her own life, no, what do you think?" The other ladies nodded, agreeing, and started whispering. One of the women was Naomi's great aunt, Fannie, who didn't love anything more than gossip, except perhaps warm bread. Better yet, warm bread and gossip together! Fannie whispered other women that of course, she knew that Naomi was dating Roy. She decided it was much better to appear that she knew things rather than to seem ignorant, even though she knew nothing about Naomi going out with that Roy boy. The other ladies began to gossip earnestly with a lack of concern about the damage that this new gossip could cause.

By the time the last piece of the barn roof was in place, everyone seemed to believe that Naomi and Roy were dating. It was amazing how fast fresh news traveled in a small Amish community, especially on the day of a barn-raising. Linda was a genius. She at least thought of herself that way, as she was more than satisfied that her plan to keep Amos and Naomi apart was already working. It appeared that the news had reached even Amos' ears. Linda watched from afar as Naomi looked to say good night to Amos. Amos had seen Naomi but after hearing the news that she was already courting another, he decided to respect her decision and decided that it was better if he did not speak to her further individually. After all, if Naomi was the respectful young lady that he thought she was, he did not want to be the one to ruin her dignity.

How was it possible though that he didn't know she was seeing someone else? Of course, a young, beautiful, intelligent, hard-working girl like Naomi would see something in Roy. Roy was, well Roy. He was charming, he had a sense of pride in his work, but there was something about Roy that Amos never really liked. He always wanted to impress the others and show off his work. A good Amish man was humble and rarely accepted praise let alone gave himself praise. Regardless, Amos thought it was better to respect Naomi's privacy, and snuck out with his family after dark without saying goodbye to Naomi. Naomi continued to scour the crowd until her mother insisted that they leave. Her mother also having heard the gossip knew that it was time to go home. What a day, she would have to speak to her daughter in private. The family just couldn't handle gossip like this. If there was any shred of truth to her daughter seeing Roy, well she should have been the first to know!

Chapter 7: Real Talk

Rebekah decided not to speak to her daughter until the next day. For certain her daughter had her the gossip too and she was worried because her little romance was discovered. And all along she had thought that her daughter was interested in the Amos King boy. Actually, Roy was not at all a suitable husband for her daughter and she simply wouldn't have it. She secretly liked the idea of her daughter marrying a King, even if it was the name only. Amos King was a nice young man and she had no reason to not let her daughter date him, except of course the fact that eventually she would be swept off her feet, and she would be all alone with a house full of boys. Even her husband was child-like sometimes and life would just not be the same without her daughter. She was hard on her daughter because she loved her, but she realized that even Naomi would want a family of her own someday. She just had hoped that it wouldn't happen quite this soon.

When dawn broke the next morning, Rebekah knocked on her daughter's bedroom door. Since she was the only girl she was lucky enough to get her own room. Privacy and all those things. Before puberty, it wasn't a problem for her to share a room with some of the boys, but now, those days were quite long gone. "Naomi, I know you're in there, come on now, this is enough, we have to talk. Naomi!" shouted Rebekah. Finally, Rebekah simply tried to door. It came open immediately and was unlocked. Naomi had already risen and was perhaps already tending to her chores. "Better," thought Rebekah, "maybe I can knock some sense into this girl!"

Rebekah marched herself toward their small barn where they kept their cow, Bella, and found Naomi in a pile on the ground, crumpled up, crying like a rag doll. "Get up! Naomi! Now!" screeched her mother. Naomi stood up and continued sobbing. "Whatever this nonsense is with Roy it stops," said Rebekah. "Understood?" she asked her daughter. "What, what?" said Naomi, finding a way to choke out a few words between the tears rolling down her face. "Roy? I don't even like Roy! He's such a rude boy! Who do you listen to these days? Me! Or everyone else?" shouted Naomi. Rebekah's mother feeling slightly bad that she had upset her daughter said, "Come inside, let's have a cup of tea. Let's go, now." Rebekah pulled her daughter off the ground and all but drug her inside the house. She then set a pot of water on the wood-burning stove and allowed Naomi to compose herself for a moment. "Let's start from the beginning," said Rebekah. "What's going on?" she asked. Naomi replied "Nothing. Except that I'm supposedly dating Roy or whatever, and yeah... I'm not ok, thanks for asking."

"Do you like that Amos boy?" asked Rebekah. "Um, yeah I think so," replied Naomi, as she slumped both further into her chair and in despair. "Well, you know, I need your help around here, Naomi, but what can I say, I can't keep you here forever. You are old enough to start dating, although, I'd be happy to keep you here as long as you'd like to stay here with me single forever!" joked Naomi's mother. "Um, Mom. That's sort of exactly what I'm afraid of, but thanks for making me feel worse, Mom," replied Naomi. "Ok, my dear, look, I do want you to be happy, you know that, right?" said Rebekah. "Yeah, I guess," answered Naomi. "Well then, don't you have some dolls to deliver?" asked Rebekah. "But, how... how do you know that I was making those dolls for Amos' cousins?" stammered Naomi. "I wasn't born yesterday my dear, I knew they had something to do with that King boy," she said. "Right, I'll be back soon," Naomi replied.

Naomi's mother watched Naomi get ready in a hurried fashion, threw her backpack over her shoulder, and flew out the door with her mother shouting something behind her that got carried away by the wind. Naomi's mother had shouted "Don't be too late for dinner!" but her words were lost on Naomi. Rebekah knew that her daughter wasn't listening, but if she wanted to date Amos King, what could she say... he was a good boy after all, and they certainly had more cows than they did, which wasn't hard to do since they had only one! Rebekah's mother chuckled to herself thinking about how her daughter was all grown up, well, almost.

Chapter 8: Doll Delivery

Naomi was almost shaking as she walked up to the door on the King's house. She hadn't announced that she was coming. It was less than 24 hours since the barn-raising, but now, for certain, everyone believed that she was dating that awful Miller boy. She had to set things straight, that she wanted to date Amos. Amos didn't answer the door when she rang the doorbell. Naomi looked up to find one of Amos' younger sisters at the door. "Moooooooom, that girl is here again," she shouted. Amos' mother, Faith King, a quiet, composed woman came to the door and asked Naomi to step inside. "Why, Naomi, you certainly have been the talk of the town, please why are you visiting us today?" asked Faith King. "Sorry, Ma'am, I just wanted to deliver something to Amos that I promised him I would make for his cousins. Can you please just give him this bag?" asked Naomi. "Better yet, why don't you step inside. Can I get you something to eat or drink?" she asked. "No Ma'am, please just tell Amos I was here," Naomi answered.

Just as Naomi turned to leave, Amos peered from behind the door. Amos didn't say anything, he just looked at her with disappointment and walked back inside the house. As Naomi turned toward the sidewalk she felt tears fall from her eyes. After Naomi had turned around and started walking away, Amos could see the sadness in her step and started to believe that he had been deceived, yet he did not call her to come back.

Inside the King's house, Faith King sat with her son Amos, like any good mother would do, and simply said, "I don't believe so much that a nice girl like Naomi would date a boy like Roy, now do you?" Having said all she needed to say, she handed her son the bag full of dolls that Naomi had made by hand for Amos' younger cousins. Amos took the bag, smiled sheepishly and plopped himself down in his favorite reading and thinking chair. He sighed a little, seeing as he did not have any younger cousins. Actually, his sister-in-law was expecting a baby in a few months, but the baby wouldn't be playing with dolls for a while. He couldn't believe how quickly he fell for her smile, her charm, her beauty. How could all of this be unfolding so terribly he thought to himself.

Chapter 9: Do or Don't

Naomi returned to her house in time for dinner, but her mother immediately knew the outcome had not been as desired. Neither Naomi nor her mother spoke about their previous discussion as dinner continued. There was a silence at the table, aside from a few requests to pass the water, the salt, and the meat. Naomi sulked all week in her home. Even when she was feeding the chickens she found herself working in complete silence when she would usually sing. You could say Amos fared worse, as he started to feel bad that he had not even received her inside the house when she arrived with the dolls that he requested her to make, nor had he offered her any jars of homemade peanut butter in exchange. One good for another. Amos worked on the farm, as usual, manual labor kept him from going a little crazy.

He found that no matter what he did his mind returned to Naomi. He was determined at the next church singing to ask to drive her home in the family's horse and buggy. The next church singing would be in three days. He knew he needed to talk to her then or he would never forgive himself. After the church service at the Stoltzfus's house, there was another church singing for the youth to gather and mingle like usual. Not even 15 minutes after the service was over, Linda found her way through the crowd to Amos.

"So, Amos, what do you know, Naomi and Roy, huh?" "Yeah, um, sure, I don't know," said Amos. "But I think they're cute together, don't you?" stated Linda, attempting to affirm her lie that Naomi and Roy were a couple. "Actually, I don't even know if they're together. I've never seen them together," he said. "Oh. Well, anyway, everyone knows they're together now," said Linda. "Ok, well, have a nice evening Linda," said Amos politely as he turned and walked away. Linda, outraged, found herself abandoned in the middle of her conversation with Amos. Her plan to ruin Naomi and Amos didn't seem to be taking hold like she thought! Wretched girl! What went wrong?

As Linda turned she saw Amos speaking with Naomi almost immediately. "Naomi, I... I don't know what came over me the other day and I'm..." Amos was cut off speaking as Linda made her way across the room towards them angrily. "Don't you know that you two are supposed to be angry at each other!!!" she yelled. All of a sudden, Linda realized that she, in fact, had just made a fool of herself. Instead of everyone looking at Amos and Naomi, or even Roy, they were all staring at Linda. Linda quickly composed herself and said, "Well, have a nice evening!"

As soon as Linda was gone from immediate sight and earshot, Amos asked Naomi, "Can I take you home tonight after the singing, if you're free?" Naomi said, "Oh, I have to ask my Mom first." "Actually, I already asked her for you, and she said yes," replied Amos. "Really?" asked Naomi. "Yes," said Amos as his cheeks grew completely red with color. "Well then, that's definitely a yes. Maybe we can sit outside on the balcony and have something to eat? Do you like to look at the stars? I love star gazing." "Sure, actually I just want to spend some time with you, if that's okay." "That would be lovely," she replied.

Amos excused himself from Naomi and mingled with some of his friends, as Naomi did the same. She found herself gleefully telling Ruth in the corner, everything that happened and how Amos was taking her home this evening. As the evening closed, Naomi waited slightly impatiently outside the gathering. The palms of her hands were sweaty just thinking about touching his hands. Amos approached her quietly, and placed the thick of his hand on the small of her back, a little too low to be only a friendly interest. Amos walked Naomi to the carriage and opened the door for to step inside. "What about your brothers and sisters?" asked Naomi, "How are they going home?" "Oh, don't worry about them, they can walk home from here," replied Amos. "So, it's just you and me then?" questioned Naomi. "It would seem so." Amos prepared the horses and they rode off into the night towards Naomi's home.

AMBER & ABEL

MONICA MARKS

<u>Amber and Abel</u>

<u>Milan, Italy</u>

"No! No! No!" Amber cried, throwing her hands up in dismay. "How did this happen? How *could* this happen?"

The others in the hung their heads in unison, no one willing to accept the blame for the most recent catastrophe.

"Giuliana is to wear the taffeta number, Gia the silk and Corina the leather and lace. Who screwed this up? Come on, speak up. Time is money, people!"

Again, only mollified silence met the designer's question.

Amber stifled a groan, knowing that she would not get an admission from the group.

"Never mind now," she sighed. "Twenty minutes to curtain. Get the models re-dressed at once. Keep an eye on the rotation! It's simple reading! It's not that complicated!"

A chorus of "yes ma'am" filled her ears and she spun to deal with the next mishap as someone shoved a clipboard in her face.

It doesn't matter how many years I've been doing this, I have yet to see a fashion show go as planned.

It was not for lack of excruciating planning of course. Every detail had been mapped to the last second months in advance and yet inevitably, someone impetrative would call in sick or a top investor would want to bring his six grandchildren backstage. Invariably, a model vomited on the runway or a make-up artist and hair stylist got into a fist fight.

It was what kept Amber's blood pressure skyrocketing and her heart rushing in her ears.

"Amber! Amber, you have an urgent phone call!"

Her assistant, Dana appeared, holding out one of the three cell phones she carried but Amber waved her away.

Every phone call was an urgent phone call. It was an occupational hazard.

"Not now, Dana. Can't you see we're T minus nineteen minutes?"

"Amber, you need to take – "

"Dana! I am up to my ears in disasters right now. Can you please deal with whatever it is? Is that not what I pay you the big bucks for?"

For a timeless second, a hush seemed to fall over the bustling backstage and inexplicably, Amber felt the hairs on her arms raise as she lifted her head.

She looked at Dana who shook her head quietly.

"What is it?" Amber breathed. "What happened?"

Dana visibly swallowed, lowering her kind, brown eyes through the lenses of her glasses.

She extended the phone further.

"It's your mother."

And Amber's world stopped.

<u>**Brooklyn, New York**</u>

"I'm looking for Leah Colville," Amber told the nurse. She drummed her fingers anxiously on the counter as the woman punched in the information and nodded.

"Room 717," she announced. "Just follow that hallway to the end."

Amber barely heard the last words as she flew down toward her mother's room.

It was slightly ajar and she pushed it open, her stomach flipping nervously.

"Mama?" she called softly. "Mama, are you awake?"

"Amber?"

She hurried inside the semi-private room, sliding the separating curtain aside.

Leah was the only one in the room but Amber knew that could change at the drop of a hat.

Oh mama, why didn't you say anything?

Her breath caught in her throat as she stared at her one virile mother, sunken in the bed, her face as white as the sterile sheets in which she lay.

Amber threw herself into her mother's arms gently.

"Oh mama," she whispered. "Why didn't you tell me it had gotten so bad?"

Leah made a dismissive sound with her tongue.

"You are a busy girl, Amber. The last thing you need is your old, sick mom crying in your ear about chemo treatments and hair loss. It's nothing you haven't heard a million times before."

Tears filled Amber's grey eyes but she hid them.

"I am never too busy for you," she scolded tenderly. "How long have you been like this?"

Leah sighed.

"Three weeks. The doctors are shocked I've hung on this long, kitten. It's only a matter of time..."

A stunning bolt of guilt almost brought Amber to her knees.

How could I not have known for three weeks? What kind of daughter am I?

"Don't talk like that!" Amber cried. "You're not going to..."

She trailed off as her voice caught in her throat.

"Shh, kitten. Don't cry now. We have both known that I have been living on borrowed time for a long while. God has been gracious enough to let me see you become successful and now I can go to the other side knowing you are secure."

Amber pursed her lips together, squeezing her mom's frail body.

"But I need you to do something for me," the older Colville woman continued and Amber raised her head.

"Anything, mama. Tell me what you need."

Leah studied her beautiful daughter's face for a long moment, reaching up to stroke her short, layered hair.

"Two things actually."

Amber stared at her expectantly.

"First, when I die, I need you to go to Pennsylvania and find my sister, Ruthie to let her know I've passed."

Amber stared at her uncomprehendingly.

"Your sister Ruthie?" she echoed. "Since when do you have a sister Ruthie?"

Leah offered her a weak smile.

"I have always had a sister, kitten."

Amber waited for her to elaborate but Leah seemed to have lost her strength suddenly.

"I'm tired, Amber," she murmured. "I would like to rest now."

"Yes, mama, of course," Amber replied, sitting up. "I will be right here when you wake up."

Leah patted her daughter's hand and smiled lovingly.

"The second thing I would like you to do it grow your hair long again. I miss those golden locks of yours."

Amber forced a smile through the tears in her eyes.

"I will do that mama. I will grow my hair and find Aunt Ruthie in Pennsylvania."

Leah nodded slowly, her eyes growing heavy.

"Just Ruthie, not Aunt Ruthie. You can find her in Eden, Pennsylvania. Ruthie Miller."

Amber watched with a trembling chin as her mother's eyes fell closed knowing that it was the last time she would ever see them open again.

Eden, Pennsylvania

Amber looked at the woman embarrassed.

"I'm afraid I don't know much more than what I've already told you," Amber admitted, wishing away the clerk's scornful scrutiny. "My mother asked me to find her sister here in Eden and I have no idea where to start."

The clerk gave her a look which was half bemused, half annoyed but she turned back to her computer.

"Ruth Miller," she sighed, shaking her head. "There has to be at least two dozen here and that's only the ones we have one record."

Amber blinked and stared at her.

"This is city hall, isn't it? Why wouldn't you have them on record? Do you have a lot of illegal immigrants here?"

Amber's question was sincere but the clerk's expression turned sardonic.

"You really are not from around here, are you?"

Amber swallowed her annoyance and forced a smile.

"No, ma'am. I am not. That is why any help you can give me would be greatly appreciated. Why would you not have someone on record?"

"This is Amish country, honey."

Amber suddenly felt foolish and she grinned sheepishly.

"Of course. Well, can you see if any of the Ruth Millers you have there have a sister named Leah?"

The clerk's red eyebrows rose almost to her hairline.

"Ruth and Leah Miller? Are you kidding me? You're definitely looking for an Amish family, sweetie."

"That can't be," Amber said shaking her head. "My mom wasn't Amish."

"Well, I can check but if it quacks like a duck…"

Again, her fingers flew over the keyboard and she raised an eyebrow.

"I have two Ruth Millers with a sibling named Leah."

She scrawled their telephone numbers onto a piece of paper for her.

"But I wouldn't get your hopes up, honey," the clerk told her as she held out the sheet. "My guess is that your Ruth Miller is somewhere in the countryside."

Amber stared at her helplessly.

"What do I do then?"

"If neither of these women is who you're seeking, I would start combing the districts."

Amber opened her mouth to ask what that meant but the older woman seemed irritated enough.

She closed her mouth and vowed to find someone else to help her find answers.

Instead, she thanked her and hurried out of the building, into the windy autumn day.

As she stood on the steps, looking down at the phone numbers in her hands, a memory flittered through her mind.

She had been about four years old and her mother pulled a long dress from a hope chest at the foot of the bed.

It had been just after Amber's father had died and Leah had been so melancholic, digging through old photos and keepsakes.

"That's an old dress, mama," Amber said, looking at the homespun fabric in awe.

"It is, kitten, yes," her mother agreed. "Would you like to try it on?"

"Yes please!" Amber cried and Leah had laughed, slipping the too large garment onto her small daughter.

The older Colville dug into the chest and removed a small white cap, placing it on the base of Amber's head.

"You look like a proper Amish girl now, *Liebchen*."

"What is an Amish girl, mama?"

"Greta!"

The voice was loud and almost directly in her ear, smashing her reverie into a million pieces.

Startled, Amber turned to look.

An Amish man stood behind her, his green eyes alight with hope as she met his stare.

"Greta, you've returned!" he said excitedly. "When did you come back to Eden?"

Amber shook her head.

"I'm sorry," she said kindly, still awed by the green of his irises. "You have me confused with someone else."

To her surprise, his brow furrowed and he scowled slightly.

"Are you playing a game?" he asked gruffly, his eyes narrowing. "You don't need to worry; I won't tell anyone I have seen you."

Amber's eyes widened and she wondered if she was in the middle of a gag.

She looked around for cameras but nothing seemed out of the ordinary.

"I really am sorry," she said again, continuing down the steps. "You have me mixed up with someone else. My name isn't Greta."

She hurried away before he could respond, leaving him staring after her.

As she made her way toward the street where her rental car waited, she glanced back uneasily at the attractive man, her heart racing.

That was strange, she thought, sliding into the driver's side.

But as she pulled away from the curb, she wondered if it was less strange and more fate.

Perhaps that man was God's way of telling her that she would find her long lost aunt inside the Amish community after all.

I guess it's time to start combing the districts, Amber thought wryly. *Whatever that means.*

She could not help but take one last peek at the man in her rear-view as she drove away. He remained standing on the steps, staring after her as if he expected her to return.

I hope he finds Greta, she thought wistfully. *He certainly seems to love her.*

"Abel, who was that?" Levi demanded, rushing up the steps of city hall to meet his brother. He peered in the direction which the car gone.

"Apparently no one," Abel muttered as he watched the small sports car zoom away from the center of town.

"From where I stood, it looked to be Greta Shetler and – "

"It was not," Abel snapped, cutting off his brother before another word could leave his lips.

Levi eyed him warily.

"You seem upset," he commented. "Hasn't that woman done enough damage to you without having you pine for her?"

"Let's not speak about her," Abel said between clenched teeth as he hurried down the steps. "We have errands to run."

Levi chuckled dryly.

"Well whoever she is, I would not mind seeing her again," Levi commented. Abel paused to give his brother a scathing look.

"She is an Englisher," he retorted. "You would do well to stay away from her."

"Why? Are you interested?" Levi mocked. "And I thought you were going to die longing for the shunned and shamed beauty of the district."

"You are speaking nonsense now, Levi," Abel chided. "If you can't speak normally, don't speak at all."

Abel didn't have to look over to know his brother was leering at him.

It seemed everyone in town had been ogling him since the day Greta had run off with the Englisher, leaving him at the altar after declaring she was pregnant with the Englisher's child.

And now she was back, pretending that she did not recognize him.

It was just another slap in the face after her ex-communication, almost two years earlier.

Has she come back to humiliate me further?

"Who was she if not Greta?" Levi demanded, obviously unwilling to leave the topic alone.

"You know you should not even be speaking her name," Abel snapped. "I don't know who that woman was."

"Then why did you run after her if you don't know her?"

Abel was growing angry with his brother's interrogation.

"Let us go our own way today. We can accomplish more that way."

Without permitting Levi an opportunity to answer, he rushed away, trying to leave his brother in his wake along with the painful memories of Greta.

After finding a quiet spot to park her car, Amber picked up her cell phone.

She tried both the phone numbers given to her by the clerk at city hall but as the woman had predicted, neither was the woman Amber sought.

Now I have to venture from district to district, she realized. She was not looking forward to the task; it seemed daunting but she knew she could not rest until she had honored her mother's wishes.

Instinctively, she reached up and touched her hair.

It had already begun to grow out some in the two months since Leah's passing and Amber was determined not to touch it.

As she drove the rental into the outskirts of Eden, the lush Pennsylvania hills fell into a smaller settlement of land and soon, she could see that she was inside the Amish district.

Almost immediately, a feeling of peace overcame her and she had to stop the car to admire the almost surreal beauty of the landscape around her.

She grabbed for her cell phone, snapping pictures as the horizon as the sun began to set over the lolling dales.

Suddenly, she heard the clopping of hooves as a wagon approached and Amber lowered her camera, watching in awe as a horse and cart ambled toward her.

In the front, a man and woman dressed in traditional Amish attire rode primly and Amber offered them a nervous smile, not knowing if she would be received with distain.

To her relief, they both returned her beam and the man slowed the beast.

"Are you lost, miss?" he asked politely and Amber shook her head.

"No...well maybe," she replied sheepishly. "I stopped to take a picture of the beautiful landscape but..."

She trailed off, suddenly embarrassed.

"I am afraid I'm on a bit of a wild goose chase," she confessed. They peered at her with curious eyes.

"Are you looking for someone's home?" the woman asked. "Perhaps we can direct you."

Amber opened her mouth to answer and then closed it.

"This is going to seem ridiculous," she muttered. "But I am looking for a woman named Ruthie Miller. Do you know her?"

The couple seemed slightly amused by the question and Amber was beginning to realize that was going to be a common response to her inquiry.

I wonder what it would be like to live in a place where everyone knew everyone else? I imagine there is a sense of security that accompanies that knowledge.

"I fear that we know several women by that name, miss. Can you tell us anything else about her?"

"She had a sister named Leah but they have been estranged for – "

Suddenly, Amber found it difficult to speak and she swallowed quickly as her voice broke.

"Have you had supper, miss?" the woman asked quietly. "Our farm is not far from here. It would be our pleasure to have you as our guest."

Amber looked up, terrified and shook her head.

"Oh no, I couldn't," she gulped. "But thank you."

The man smiled.

"It is considered very rude to refuse a supper invitation in Amish country," he informed her and Amber could see he was teasing her but all the same, she found herself nodding.

"That would be lovely," she breathed. "Thank you."

"You may follow us," the woman said, smiling.

Amber nodded and allowed them to pass before jumping back into her car.

What lovely people, she thought, her heart warming. The man on the steps of city hall had made her nervous and so far, he had been the only interaction she had with anyone in their culture.

But he did have lovely green eyes.

Amber steered the Chrysler into up the long drive of the pretty farmhouse, keeping a safe distance behind the kind strangers.

Slowly, she exited her car, suddenly aware of how strange was what she was doing.

Would I ever accept such an unexpected dinner invitation from random strangers in New York or Milan or Paris? Of course not. So why am I doing it here?

The answer was obvious; it felt right.

She was nowhere near any major city, designing clothes and fighting with stage hands or arguing with models.

It was like she had entered another world, another planet even where Amber Colville didn't exist and she was just a lost little girl, looking for the last family relation she had left in the world.

Does my Aunt Ruthie have children? Maybe I have cousins out there. Or should I say, in here.

"Come along, miss. It's growing cold without the sun shining down on us," the woman urged.

"My name is Amber," she volunteered as she was led into the house. "Amber Colville."

The wife smiled and nodded.

"That is a lovely name. I am Beth and that is my husband, Jeremiah Troyer."

"Pleased to meet you, Mr. and Mrs. Troyer," I said politely.

She smiled softly.

"We do not use such formalities here. You may call us Beth and Jeremiah," she said softly.

Amber blushed lightly and nodded.

"Only if you call me Amber," she agreed.

"Please, come and sit. Our boys should be along shortly. They have been commissioned with supper as Jeremiah and I were in town today."

"I see," she said, nodding. "But you are farmers?"

"Yes," Beth replied. "We grow wheat and barley. Our boys have recently acquired chickens but between you and I, Amber, I am rather fearful of their pecking beaks."

Amber chuckled with Jeremiah.

"There is no shame in having fears, Beth," her husband said, reassuringly. "I am certain even the English have fears."

Amber's smile broadened.

"Oh yes," she assured them. "More fears than I care to admit."

A sudden warmth flowed between them as they stood in a comfortable silence.

"Come along inside," Jeremiah said, shooing them from the foyer. "I will see about some cider. It is cooling in the shed. Abel just made a fresh batch."

"He's a good boy, our eldest," Beth murmured but Amber noticed a dark cloud cross over her eyes as if something occurred to her.

She stared at Amber, her mouth parting slightly.

"Is something wrong, Beth?" Amber asked, immediately concerned by her change of disposition.

The older woman shook her head.

"I will help Jeremiah with the cider. The barrel can be difficult to manage. Please, sit by the fire until we return."

She was gone before Amber could reply and she was abruptly filled with a small fission of alarm.

That was strange, she thought but she was ashamed of her suspicion. *Things are just done differently here than they are in the city. There's nothing strange about it.*

"*Mamm! Daed?*"

She turned her head as a man called out, poking his head into the sitting room where Amber had sunk into a wing chair.

He seemed to freeze as he looked at her.

"Hello," Amber volunteered. "I'm Amber Colville. Your parents have invited me for dinner."

A small smile appeared on the young man's lips and he stalked toward her, extending his hand.

"Levi Troyer," he announced. "You were in Eden today, were you not?"

Surprised, Amber nodded.

"Yes, I was at city hall, looking for information."

Levi's eyebrow raised.

"What sort of information?" he asked curiously, placing himself into the chair facing her.

Amber swallowed and shook her head.

"It's not really important," she said quickly. "I would rather not get into it right now."

Levi's blue eyes narrowed slightly.

"I can be a wonderful source of information," he told her. "If you ever feel like talking."

His meaning was unmistakable and Amber found herself amused and slightly intrigued by the forward speaking man.

"Thank you," she replied, laughing. "Perhaps after dinner. It's not a very cheerful supper conversation."

"Levi, why did you leave me alone to finish supper. I have – "

Amber turned toward the doorway again and her jaw dropped.

"Wh -what is she doing here?" the man gasped, looking accusingly at his brother. Levi jumped to his feet, grinning.

"It appears as thought *Mamm* and *Daed* have invited her over for supper. Amber, this is my brother, Abel."

Cautiously, Amber rose to her feet, unsure of how Abel would react to her as she recalled their previous encounter.

"Hello Abel," she said quietly. "Pleased to meet you."

She wasn't sure if she should extend her hand or not but she found herself once more staring into his impossibly green eyes as if hypnotized.

He did not immediately respond and Amber felt her heart sink slightly as he continued to stare at her.

"Forgive my brother," Levi interceded. Amber turned questioningly to him.

"He seems to think you look like someone he knew once a long time ago," Levi offered and Amber nodded slightly.

"I never said that," Abel grumbled but Amber felt that his gaze betrayed his words. He could not seem to pull his irises from her face as if trying to memorize every feature.

"There you are," Beth said, hurrying into the front room, a concerned expression on her face. She held out a glass for Amber.

"This is apple cider from the Bachman's orchid," she told Amber, smiling briefly. The older woman seemed to sense the tension in the room.

"I see you have met our sons, Abel and Levi," she continued as Amber accepted the cup. "What have you made for supper, boys? I am sure our guest is as hungry as your father."

"What did the doctor say, *Mamm*?" Abel asked suddenly, diverting his attention to his mother.

Beth's face turned pale and angry.

"Abel, that is hardly an appropriate question to ask before visitors. Go tend to supper," she snapped with a harshness Amber was sure was not customary.

Abel seemed contrite but he disappeared, bowing his head somewhat shamefully.

Amber felt a spark of apprehension in her stomach as she cast Beth a sidelong look.

Why did she go to the doctor? Is she ill? Does she have cancer like mama?

Amber bit on her lower lip and tried to push the image of her mother from her mind but it was more difficult than she wished.

"Are you all right, Amber?" Beth asked, her brow furrowing deeper as she watched the blonde's face crumble.

Amber tried to nod but a tear escaped her and slid down her cheek.

"I'm sorry," the younger woman told the others, quickly wiping the streak from her face. "I recently lost my mother and I was just thinking of her. Forgive me for my display."

Beth and Levi made a commiserating noise.

"Levi, go help your brother and leave the women to talk," Beth ordered. Levi rose without protest, leaving them alone in the front room.

"It is difficult to lose a parent," Beth said comfortingly. "I have lost both of mine."

Amber sighed.

"I am so sorry, Beth. My father also died when I was very young."

Beth leaned down to pat her hand soothingly and Amber found the gesture heartwarming.

I am a perfect stranger to her and yet she feels the need to comfort me. This place is like a television program. This isn't real life. This is a place where daughters would know that their mothers have been dying for weeks, not off running fashion shows in Italy.

"Supper is ready, *Mamm*, Amber," Levi called from the dining room and the women rose to join the others at the dinner table.

"We pray before eating, Amber. You are not required to join us," Jeremiah told her as she took a seat across from the Troyer brothers.

"I would be happy to join in your prayer if you'll have me," Amber replied. She pretended not to notice the look of appreciation shared by the family as she hung her head.

Jeremiah lead the prayer in Pennsylvania Dutch but Amber could catch some of the key words from the time she had spent in Munich.

"You still have not told us what you are doing in our district, Gre – ah, Amber," Levi piped up after they had loaded their plates with meat, vegetables, potatoes and bread.

Beth and Jeremiah looked up sharply while Abel's jaw tightened.

"Were you going to call me Greta also?" Amber asked, her eyes widening. Levi seemed embarrassed.

"You do bear an uncanny resemblance to her," he confessed.

"I did not notice," Beth interjected, eyeing her older son.

"Nor did I!" Jeremiah agreed and there was a finality in his tone. It was clear that the subject was to be dropped and Amber did not want to push the issue.

Nevertheless, she was fascinated by the fact she might have an Amish twin.

"I have come here looking for my mother's sister but I'm afraid I don't have much to go off. I don't even know if I'm looking in the right spot but my mom only told me about her before she died."

Beth looked up and smiled.

"We told Amber we would happily help her find her aunt but we would need to narrow the search somehow."

"What is her name?"

Amber was surprised it was Abel who asked the question.

"Ruthie Miller. Her sister, my mother, was Leah."

The table fell silent as the family appeared to rake their memories.

"Well, I can think of four women by that name. One is far too young to be your aunt, one is much too old and the other two have lived in the district all their lives without a sister named Leah," Jeremiah volunteered, chewing his fried steak pensively. "Have I forgotten someone?"

"No...I do not believe you have," Beth replied. She gazed at her boys.

"Any suggestions?"

Levi shrugged his shoulders.

"As Amber has said, there is no guarantee that this Ruthie Miller is from this district. Perhaps I could take her to the neighboring districts tomorrow and we could investigate further."

He beamed at her and Amber smiled back but she could not help her gaze from falling on the older Troyer brother.

He seemed to glower into his plate, unspeaking.

"That would be lovely," Amber said reluctantly, realizing that Abel was not about to volunteer his help.

Is he always so brooding or is it because I remind him of this Greta?

"It's settled then. Tomorrow I will take you in search of your aunt!" Levi said jovially.

Amber could not help but notice that he gently jabbed his brother in the ribs and she wondered if she hadn't put herself in the middle of a sibling rivalry.

Abel could not sleep and he lay on his back, arms folded across his chest.

"I can feel you breathing fire over there, Abe," Levi called mockingly through the dark. "Why are you so upset?"

"I'm not!" Abel denied but Levi only laughed.

"Why don't you just admit that you want to take Amber on her search tomorrow?"

"I do not," he replied hotly but as he said the words, he knew they were a lie.

He couldn't seem to get over the remarkable likeness Amber shared to Greta. It was as if *Gotte* had sent him a chance to get things right with Greta.

That's ridiculous. They are two different women. If Levi wishes to waste his time with an Englisher, let him do it.

"You truly are a fool," Levi sighed, sitting up. Abel turned his head to scowl at his brother in the moonlit room.

"You would know a fool to see one, brother," he snapped. "Stop talking and let me go to sleep."

Levi groaned.

"I only offered to take Amber tomorrow because I knew you wouldn't. You will pick her up at her hotel in Eden and take her."

"I will not!" Abel was insulted at the idea of stealing his brother's date. "She has agreed to go with you, not me."

"But she wants to go with you," Levi insisted. "She could not stop staring at you all through dinner. Didn't you notice?"

Abel had not.

"Of course you didn't notice. You were too busy sulking about Greta to notice the lovely woman yearning for you to look at her. I think Amber is *Gotte's* way of telling you that it is time to move on."

"What do you know?" Abel growled but in his heart, he felt a sliver of hope.

Is he just telling me that because he believes I have spent too much time pining over Greta or did Amber find me interesting?

"I know that if you don't act on this opportunity, I will give you no more second chances. I will pursue Amber myself."

Abel didn't answer but his heart sank at his brother's words.

Maybe this is a sign from Gotte. What harm can it do to take her tomorrow?

Amber felt a spark of happiness when she saw Abel at the reins the following morning in front of the Eden Resort and Suites.

"I hope you do not mind that I have come in my brother's place," Abel said, somewhat gruffly but Amber was already learning that it was shyness, not rudeness.

"I am very happy it was you," she replied earnestly, catching his eye.

A shiver coursed down her spine as he helped her onto the wagon and they made their way out of town toward the districts.

She found herself studying his handsome profile, taking in the fine shape of his nose and delicate bone structure.

"I hope that you will not be disappointed," Abel told her as they started their ride in silence.

Amber glanced at him in surprise, thinking that he had caught her staring at him.

She blushed and shook her head.

"I'm not disappointed in the least," she replied, lowering her eyes.

He shot her a sidelong look and gave her a lopsided smile.

"I meant that I hope you find your aunt," he explained. Amber turned bright red and cleared her throat in nervousness.

"Of course," she muttered, doubly ashamed.

She had almost forgotten the reason for their drive as if they were merely on a date.

Focus on the task at hand, she told herself.

Soon, they were in one of the neighboring districts and Abel proved to be a wonderful guide, finding a minister to question almost immediately.

They did not find anyone to match their description in the first two districts they visited but as they made their way into the third, it was growing late in the afternoon and Amber was growing disheartened.

"I'm beginning to think this is a lost cause," Amber confessed as they searched for the home of the deacon as directed by a young girl playing hopscotch.

Despite her mounting disappointment, she could not shake the idyllic beauty of their community.

I would give it all up to live here, she thought as they found Deacon Roth tending to his herb garden.

"Hello, Deacon," Abel called. "I am Abel Troyer and this is my friend, Amber. We have some questions for you if you have a moment."

The deacon looked up and nodded, smiling welcomingly.

"Of course," he agreed. "What can I help you with?"

"Deacon, have you a Ruthie Miller who lives here? She would be in her forties or fifties with an estranged sister named Leah?"

The elderly man's mouth parted and he stared at Amber for a long moment.

"Indeed," he murmured. "Are you Ruthie's daughter?"

Amber shook her head.

"No...I am Leah's daughter," Amber replied, glancing nervously at Abel. "Do you know them?"

The man nodded thoughtfully.

"Of course, I remember Leah. She never was baptized. She fell in love with an Englisher and married him when she was nineteen or so."

Amber nodded excitedly.

"Yes! Alexander Colville. That was my father," Amber gushed. "Is Ruthie still here?"

"No, child. Ruthie was married to a man named Samuel Miller but he died in a terrible accident not two years after the wedding. That was about a year after Leah had left the district."

Amber found her palms sweating and she wiped them on her jeans.

"Where did she go? Did my aunt leave the community too?"

The deacon chuckled.

"No, no. She eventually remarried and moved on to another district."

"Nearby?" Amber pressed, her excitement mounting.

I'm so close to finding your sister, mama! She thought, her heart racing.

"Yes, two districts across."

Abel's face turned confused.

"Closest to Eden?" he asked and the older man nodded.

"But that's our district," Abel murmured. A look of understanding crossed his face.

"Who did she marry when she moved?" he asked.

The deacon thought for a long moment, digging into the depth of his swiss cheese memory bank.

"Ah yes. David Shetler. As far as I know, they still live there but I confess, I am out of touch sometimes," Deacon Roth chortled.

Abel's face turned grey.

"Do you know these people, Abel?" Amber asked excitedly. "Do you know where I can find them?"

He looked at her, his face aghast.

"Yes," he whispered. "I know them. They are Greta's parents. You are Greta's cousin."

The ride back to Eden was long and quiet as Abel tried to gather his thoughts. To his relief, Amber did not push him to speak as if she could sense he needed the quiet.

Is this a cruel joke? Sending me a cousin of the woman who broke my heart? One who looks so much like her?

But as they continued the journey back, Abel suddenly realized that he had been blinded by Amber's outward appearance.

True, she looked like Greta with the solemn grey eyes as sunny blonde hair but how similar were the two really?

Greta could not seem to run away fast enough, sacrificing her own values to do so while Amber embraced her mother's home and heritage in tribute.

Greta was selfish and hurtful while Amber was kind and loving.

Greta was gone and Amber was right there beside him, waiting for him to speak, to make the next step.

"It is getting late," he finally told her. "I don't think it is wise to interrupt your aunt at this hour although I am certain she will be happy to see you, regardless of the time."

Amber nodded but he could see the sadness in her eyes.

"That's fine. I can find my own way there tomorrow," she replied, trying to sound cheerful. "But I appreciate all your help."

She turned her head quickly but he knew it was only so he wouldn't see the tears in her eyes.

He paused, searching for the next words to say.

Opening his mouth, his perfectly concocted statement flew into the air.

"I am hungry," he said instead.

Amber turned to glance at him.

"You're hungry?" she repeated. "Oh."

She wasn't quite sure what to make of the statement.

"Me too," she replied suddenly.

Their eyes met and they smiled.

"May I buy you dinner, Amber?" he asked her sweetly.

"Like a date?" she teased.

His smiled faded and he nodded solemnly.

"Exactly like a date," he replied.

AN AMISH HOMECOMING

STEPHANIE SWIFT

David Montgomery walked the aisles of Alexander Mercantile & Grocery, shuffling about aimlessly while country music streamed from the overhead speakers. He'd picked up several items and given them the once-over before putting them back on the shelves with a dissatisfied grunt. If he were visiting a hardware store or lumber yard, this shopping trip would be a breeze, but trying to decide which brand of flour to buy for his mother's chicken pot pie recipe? He didn't have a clue.

He closed his eyes and groaned again. There was only one logical way to choose, but before he could eenie-meenie-miney-moe his way through it, he heard the soft sound of laughter from someone close by. David turned to find a young woman dressed in Amish clothing standing a few feet away, sorting through a shelf lined with oils and spices.

Peeking from beneath her white bonnet was a head full of long red hair, which was gathered at the nape of her neck with a blue ribbon. The bright red shade was a shocking contrast to her milky complexion and light blue eyes and gave her the appearance of a porcelain doll. The beautiful resemblance left him momentarily speechless, and when she walked over and picked up a small bag of flour and put it in his cart, he forced himself to stop gawking at her like a smitten teenager.

"If you're shopping for Miss Rosemary, you better get this brand or she'll tan your hide."

The mention of his mother's name brought him back to reality. It shouldn't have surprised him, given that there was only one Amish community in the vicinity – the same one his mother belonged to – and everyone knew each other by name.

"I apologize for the intrusion. I live a couple of houses down from Miss Rosemary," she said. "I'm Faith Somers."

She held out her hand, and David cleared his throat as he shook her hand and forced a smile. He noticed right away how soft and smooth her skin was, but her handshake was unusually firm and a lot like most of the men he'd met, which caught him off guard.

"David Montgomery. It's nice meeting you."

She nodded. "I recognized you from your photo. Miss Rosemary brags on you all the time."

David's thoughts flashed to the framed pictures of him his mother kept in her living room, and he felt his cheeks heat. They ranged from ages one to eighteen, and each year was more embarrassing than the one before.

"Well, I'll let you get back to your shopping. Have a blessed day, Mr. Montgomery!"

Before he had the chance to reply, she brushed past him and continued down the aisle without another glance in his direction. When she turned the corner and disappeared, David furrowed a brow. *Mr. Montgomery?* He hadn't heard that endearment since Bishop Luke presided over his father's funeral two years prior. Just how old did Faith Somers think he was?

David gathered the remaining items on his mother's shopping list and made his way to the checkout counter. He'd been in Dayton only three days, and he'd already talked to more people from the small Amish village than he could ever recall from the short time he lived there. So much for staying under the radar.

As an elderly gentleman scanned his groceries, David's gaze went to the large bulletin board on the wall behind the counter where several classified ads were posted. One in particular, with the headline CARPENTER NEEDED, caught his attention. The flyer's edges were tattered and worn, and the paper was faded, giving him the impression it had been on the board for quite some time.

"Excuse me, but do you happen to know the person who posted that ad?"

He pointed to the flyer in question, and when the cashier glanced at it, he shook his head. "Carson Andrews," he replied. "He was needing someone to help built a fence around his property, but that was a couple of months ago. Haven't seen him in here since then, so I don't know if he still needs the help or not."

When the man gave him his change and receipt, David scribbled the phone number from the flyer on the back of it. With any luck, the job would still be available. It wouldn't hurt to give it a shot.

"If you're looking for work, I might have something for you."

David turned toward the familiar voice and found Faith Somers standing behind him. As he folded the receipt and stuffed it inside the breast pocket of his shirt, she began unloading her shopping basket onto the counter. She stood so close he could almost count every one of her long, beautiful eyelashes.

David took a cautious step backward. "What did you have in mind?"

She smiled at him, and he could just barely make out the indention of dimples in her cheeks, which he had to admit was rather adorable.

"I inherited my grandfather's house when he passed away last year, and I've been meaning to hire someone to renovate the kitchen cabinets. Would you be interested?"

The thought of being in close quarters with a beauty like Faith intrigued him but also made him a little leery. After leaving the Amish way of life and starting over in a different city several miles away, the last thing he needed was someone or something tempting him to stay. Then again, for all he knew she might be married. If that was the case, then he was being ridiculous for no reason.

"Sounds good to me. When should I start?"

The cashier bagged her groceries and as Faith looped the handles over her right arm, he caught the elderly man watching them with an amused look on his face.

"Can you come by tomorrow morning, say around 9:00?"

He agreed, and as Faith made her way to the exit, he turned to look at the cashier, who was still smiling like a kid who'd been caught with his hand in a cookie jar.

"Do you know something I don't?" he asked.

The man looked down at the floor and chuckled before peering at David over his eyeglasses and giving him a look that teetered on the brink of sympathy. "All I'm going to say is good luck because I have a feeling you're going to need it."

With that, he turned and walked toward the back of the store. He never stopped laughing, and David couldn't help but wonder what he'd just gotten himself into.

He frowned. Perhaps he shouldn't have accepted the job so hastily, but unfortunately, there was no turning back now.

* * * *

The next morning, Faith put her hands on her hips and gave the kitchen faucet a resentful glare. She'd spent the past hour trying to replace the outdated equipment, but so far, the rusty nuts and bolts wouldn't budge. She gazed at her surroundings and let out a resigned sigh. Since the day she'd moved into her grandfather's old farmhouse, she'd been met with one obstacle after another. The ornery faucet shouldn't have come as much of a surprise, but it was more of an annoyance than anything. For once, she just wished something would go smoothly.

A loud knock on the front door startled Faith as she wiped the sweat from her brow and attempted to smooth the wrinkles on the front of her dress. She knew she probably looked a fright after her tug-of-war with the faucet, but at the moment she was too irritated to care what David Montgomery thought of her appearance.

Faith rolled her eyes heavenward. No, that wasn't the truth. After meeting him the day before, she hadn't been able to concentrate on anything else, so she actually cared a little bit too much what he might think of her.

She tucked a couple of wayward tendrils behind her ears and took a deep breath before opening the front door. David stood on the other side with a toolbox in one hand and a plate of cookies wrapped in plastic wrap in the other. It was odd seeing an English man standing on her front porch, and the sight of one in jeans and a t-shirt made her heart thump a little faster.

"Mom wouldn't let me leave the house without these, so I hope you like oatmeal cookies."

When he handed her the plate, their fingers grazed for a split second, but it was enough to make the tiny hairs on the back of her neck stand at attention. She stepped to the side to let him enter, and when he walked inside, she caught the faint scent of his cologne – a woodsy, masculine scent that tickled her senses and made her knees tremble.

"I love anything Miss Rosemary cooks," she replied. "Thank you."

As they stood facing each other in the tiny den, she was immediately struck by how tall and broad-shouldered he was. He looked larger than life, especially given their close proximity, and Faith tried in vain not to stare. When he suddenly closed the small gap between them and pressed his fingers against her right cheek, she thought for certain her heart would pound right out of her chest.

"You've got something on your cheek," he remarked. "Is that rust?"

He gently wiped the smudge away, and the heat from his touch made her light-headed as she cleared her throat and nodded.

"I've been trying to replace the kitchen faucet, and it hasn't been going very well."

She used his question as a chance to flee from the close quarters of the den and into a different room with more space to move around – and less room for touching. The kitchen was the largest room in the house, and as she motioned for him to follow her, she stayed two steps ahead of him and remained at arm's length as much as possible.

David placed his toolbox on the dining room table and looked around the room. "I see the problem," he replied with a grin. "These cabinets look like they rolled in with the Titanic."

His whole face lit up every time he smiled, and it was quite endearing and made the butterflies flip-flop inside her stomach.

"Everything in this house is ancient," she said. "I'm afraid it's going to take forever to renovate it the way I want to."

David opened his toolbox and took out a wrench, which he used to loosen the nuts and bolts on the kitchen faucet. After fighting with it for over an hour, Faith was dumbfounded when he had it completely taken apart in less than five minutes.

"There we go. Now, where is the new one?"

Faith shook her head as she placed the oatmeal cookies on a metal rack inside the refrigerator. "David, I appreciate the help, but you don't have to worry with that."

He shooed her comment away with a wave of his hand. "I don't mind. I bought an old ranch house that was in foreclosure when I moved away from here, so I know how time-consuming it can be. I'm happy to help."

Faith retrieved her shopping bag from Alexander Mercantile and pulled out the box containing the new faucet fixture. When she handed it over to David, he took to the task like a duck to water while she sat down at the dining room table and made mental notes for the other fixtures that needed replacing.

"Were you able to sell it?" she asked.

He stopped for a moment and gave her a quizzical look. "My house? Why would I do that?"

Faith was confused. From everything she'd been told, David had moved back permanently to care for his mother, but perhaps she'd misunderstood somehow.

"I'm sorry. I thought you were planning on staying here with Miss Rosemary."

David gave her a half-hearted smile, but he didn't reply right away, so she watched in silence as he tightened the bolts on the new fixture and made some other small adjustments before returning his wrench to the toolbox.

"I work in Franklin with the local fire department, and I just took a temporary leave of absence. I hope I'll be able to go back within the next two or three weeks."

For reasons she couldn't explain, his remark bothered her a lot more than she cared to admit. She wanted to say it was because she hated seeing Miss Rosemary living alone, but she knew that was only partly true. Maybe it was just her imagination, but she could have sworn there was a spark, an attraction – *something* – between the two of them, but perhaps it was one-sided. What did she know anyway? She couldn't even remember the last time a man flirted with her.

Faith stood and stuffed her hands inside her dress pockets. "I was hoping these cabinets could be painted white and the hinges and knobs replaced with something more modern. Do you think that's doable?"

He seemed taken aback by the sudden change in conversation, but she couldn't see wasting any more time on something that was unlikely to happen. If only she'd known his plans before offering him a job. With any luck, she wouldn't have to babysit him while he worked and she could stay busy doing her own thing – away from him.

David opened a couple of the cabinets and inspected the wood by running his fingertips along the grain. "It would take some sanding and a couple coats of primer, but I think they would look great painted."

Faith muddled through the next thirty minutes or so in a daze as they discussed color options and how long it would take to finish the job. She focused on other things in the room while they talked so she wouldn't be forced to concentrate on his piercing green eyes and the way his muscles flexed every time he moved.

When the details were sorted through, and David started working by removing the cabinet doors, she couldn't escape the house fast enough. Fortunately, she had chores to tend to outside that would keep her busy most of the day. As Faith closed the front door behind her and started the short trek to the barn, she whispered a silent plea for God to make the next two weeks go by as quickly as possible.

* * * *

David heard the commotion as soon as he walked outside, and he shook his head and laughed as he started for Faith's barn. The disgruntled groans and language that bordered on the obscene had become a common occurrence over the past two weeks, but no matter how hard he tried to help Faith with her chores, she always stubbornly refused.

David peeked his head inside the door, and he stifled another laugh as he watched her trying to milk one of the heifers. The animal was tied to a stall, and each time Faith leaned forward to grab onto her teats, the heifer would move just out of her reach. When Faith leaned over too far and fell sideways off the short wooden stool she was sitting on, David decided it was time to intervene before her temper got the best of her.

Before he could reach her, however, she kicked the stool several feet away and let out another frustrated groan that startled the heifer and rattled the tin roof.

"Whoa!" he exclaimed. "What was that about?"

He picked up the stool and brought it back to her, and he bit his tongue so he wouldn't laugh again when he discovered her sitting cross-legged on the ground with her arms staunchly crossed over her chest. She'd taken off her bonnet, and her lovely face was almost the same shade as her bright red hair. She looked like she could spit nails, and he approached her much like he did the bull in his mother's pasture – cautiously and with no sudden movements.

"I give up!" she yelled. "This cow hates me."

David set the stool down in front of her and sat down on it. "I seriously doubt that. I think she's just stubborn – kind of like someone else I know."

She flashed him a look of contempt, but he didn't waver, and they sat there in their own little battle of wills until Faith's shoulders slumped and she bowed her head.

"I don't know what I'm doing wrong. Nothing has gone right since I moved here last year. I'm starting to think I'm cursed or something."

Her voice was soft and sullen, and she looked so pitiful it made his heart ache. He wanted to console her somehow, but he had to fight the urge to take her in his arms.

"Faith, you're not cursed. I don't think you're giving yourself enough credit. I've seen how hard you work to keep this place running smoothly, and you're doing a great job. I'm sure your grandfather would be proud."

She looked up at him, and he caught a shimmer of tears in the corners of her eyes seconds before she wiped them away with her dress sleeve. If he'd learned anything in the past two weeks, it was that Faith Somers didn't want anyone seeing just how vulnerable she could be. He admired her tenacity, but sometimes he felt it did her more harm than good.

"I wish you would let me help you," he remarked.

It wasn't the first time he'd made such a request. He offered his help with the chores repeatedly, but she was adamant about doing everything herself. Faith was the most independent and stubborn woman he'd ever met, and it was admirable as much as it was irritating.

"David, I grew up with four brothers and no sisters, so I've spent most of my life trying to prove myself. My family has always treated me like a fragile wallflower, and sometimes I really believe that's why my grandfather willed this place to me. We were very close, and he knew how much I hated living in my brother's shadows."

It was the first time she'd opened up to him about something personal, and David was almost afraid to move or even breathe. He didn't want to ruin the moment, so he remained as quiet as a church mouse.

"When my family visits, it feels like they're watching and judging everything I do, so I have to stay on my toes all the time and make sure everything is perfect. It can be very tiring. I would love to have just one day to relax on my front porch with a cup of coffee and a good book."

David got off the stool and patted it with his hand. She sounded so downtrodden it was breaking his heart, and he was determined to help her in some way, even if she fought him kicking and screaming.

"What?" she asked.

She straightened her spine and was immediately on the defensive, as usual. Undeterred, David pat the stool again. "Come on. We're going to do this together, and you can either do it willingly, or I'll sit here and wait as long as I need to."

It didn't take as long as he expected it would, and with another one of her agitated groans, she sat down on the stool while he stood and took hold of the rope tied loosely around the heifer's neck. He coaxed the animal into position beside Faith before rubbing his hands over her head and down her neck.

"Now, I want you gently rub her stomach," he directed.

Faith crossed her arms over her chest again and gave him an incredulous look. "You can't be serious."

David tried to be as stern with her as he could. "You can attract more flies with honey than vinegar. Would you want someone with an attitude touching you?"

His question made her blush, and David immediately wished he'd worded the question differently. He didn't mean for it to come out sounding as flirty as it did, but she wasn't frowning anymore, so that was something. Faith placed her small hands against the heifer's stomach and moved them around in slow circles.

"She needs to feel like she can trust you, so take your time and don't rush," he whispered. "Rubbing her fur will help warm your hands too. They don't care for cold hands when it comes to milking."

He was trying to explain the technique as delicately as possible, so as not to offend her, but her cheeks reddened again. He felt like he should apologize, but before he had the opportunity, Faith started humming a soft tune and caught him off guard. He didn't recognize the song, but it was quite beautiful and seemed to lull the animal into submission.

David kept a firm grip on the rope while Faith placed a metal bucket under the heifer and began milking her. She continued humming throughout the entire process and the animal never flinched or tried to move away. He had to admit he was impressed. She stole a glance in his direction and when she flashed him a genuine smile, his heart thumped wildly inside his chest. When the bucket was full, she moved it out of the way and stood up slowly so as not to startle the heifer. She caressed the animal's back for several minutes, and when she stopped and took a step back, David felt like breaking into a raucous round of applause.

"That was amazing!" he exclaimed. "Well done!"

He noticed she stood a little straighter and jutted her chin out, like she was pleased with her accomplishment, and the change in her demeanor made him smile.

"Thank you, David. Your guidance made all the difference."

He could tell by the tone of her voice that it was a sincere compliment, and he swallowed past the lump in his throat before attempting to reply.

"You did the work. I'm proud of you."

An awkward silence followed, and David used the opportunity to untie the heifer and lead her to one of the empty stalls while Faith took the bucket and placed it on a table near the barn door. When he peeked over the stall, he caught her fretting with her dress and hair like she was trying to make herself presentable, and the sight made him smile.

David latched the gate and walked over to join her. "I finished installing the last of the hardware in the kitchen. Would you like to see it?"

For some strange reason, her attitude changed as soon as he asked. He didn't understand why, but her smile faded and she gave him a half-hearted nod instead of replying. He picked up the bucket of milk and followed her outside, but she kept her gaze locked on the large open field behind the house instead of speaking to him during the short walk.

When they made their way inside to the kitchen, he put the bucket on the dining room table and stood quietly by as she moved from one cabinet to the next, inspecting his work. She made the decision to go with a beige paint color instead of white, and he was glad she did because it gave the whole room a cozy and comfortable feel that was very inviting.

"Everything looks wonderful, David."

Her voice was low and solemn, and his curiously finally got the best of him. "Faith, did I say something wrong? You seem upset."

She turned to look at him, and he didn't know if it was real or simply for his own benefit, but she squared her shoulders and gave him a big smile. "I'm sorry. I guess I'm just tired," she replied. "I really appreciate your hard work over the past couple of weeks. It's beautiful."

She broke their gaze and looked at the cabinets again, and he still wasn't convinced she was telling the truth, but he didn't want to keep prying and risk making her angry. When he started gathering his supplies, she picked up his hammer beside the kitchen sink and placed it inside his toolbox.

"So, I guess you'll be heading back to Franklin soon?"

David shrugged. "I suppose so. Mom keeps hinting that she's ready for me to leave. I've taken care of everything on her to-do list, and I think she misses her peace and quiet."

He chuckled when he said it, but Faith either didn't think it was funny or she didn't hear a word he said, because her expression never changed. Their hands touched as he closed the toolbox, and the warmth of her skin sent an electric jolt to the tips of his toes. She glanced at him for a brief moment before turning and walking over to one of the kitchen drawers, where she removed a thick white envelope.

"Thank you so much for your help, David. I believe this is the amount we agreed on."

She handed him the envelope and stood by silently, as if waiting for him to count the money in front of her, but he put it in his back pocket instead. Honestly, he would have done the job for free if she'd let him. Being able to spend time with her was all the compensation he needed.

"Do you mind if I come by and see you before I leave?" he asked.

He expected her to say no, but he was pleasantly surprised when she said yes. He wanted more than anything to wrap his arms around her and pull her close, but instead he tenderly kissed her cheek. He hoped she might turn her head at the last second so he could kiss her lips, but she never moved a muscle.

Disappointed, David picked up his toolbox and left for home.

* * * *

Faith steered the tractor toward the barn and uttered a plea to the Lord for the ancient machine to make it there. For the past two hours she'd listened to it choke and sputter as she tried to get some work done in the field, and it lasted solely on a wing and a prayer. As she neared the barn, she caught sight of David traveling down the main road in Miss Rosemary's wagon, and she waved as he drew closer. Her heart raced uncontrollably, but it wasn't something she wasn't used to – especially when David was around.

She knew from the gossip filtering through the community that he was leaving for Franklin later that afternoon, and she hoped he was coming by to see her like he said he would. It was a moment she'd been looking forward to and dreading at the same time. She'd barely slept since the day he left after completing his work on the kitchen cabinets. She'd even contemplated finding some other job he could do that might keep him in town just a little while longer.

Faith managed to get the tractor a few feet from the barn before it started sputtering again, and she let out a yelp and covered her eyes when her line of vision was suddenly obscured by sparks shooting from the engine. She parked the tractor and killed the motor, but within a matter of seconds the engine was engulfed in flames.

Faith scrambled off the tractor and raced toward the well just as David came careening into her driveway. He'd barely brought the wagon to a complete stop before he was jumping over the side and rushing to help her. Everything happened so quickly she barely had time to catch her breath, but they were able to douse the fire with three buckets of water from the well before the flames reached the barn.

As Faith watched the last few puffs of smoke billow from the engine, she sat on the ground and pulled her knees toward her chest. She fought it valiantly, but her tears won in the end, and as they streamed down her cheeks she didn't try to stop them. It was all too much to handle, and she was so tired of the constant struggle. Maybe it was time to give up and let one of her brothers take over the farm. They hounded her about it constantly. Maybe this was a sign from God that she was meant to do something else.

David sat down beside her, but he didn't say anything, and for that she was grateful. She didn't want sympathetic words or to be coddled like a child. She wanted to be left alone to cry until she had nothing left. She wanted to drain every last teardrop from her body and soul and just get it over with once and for all.

They sat in silence for a long time, even after Faith stopped crying and settled down. When she glimpsed in his direction, she caught him looking at her with a big smile on his handsome face. He pulled a handkerchief from his pants pocket, and his amused expression never wavered.

"Feel better?" he asked.

If he was trying to annoy her, it was working, and as Faith jerked the handkerchief from his hand, she glared at him spitefully.

"Yes, as a matter of fact. I do feel better. I've seen the light, and I realize now that I'm not meant to do this, so I can finally move on with my life."

David scooted closer to her, and when there was barely an inch remaining between them, she held her breath expectantly.

"And here I was thinking you did this intentionally to try and keep me from leaving," he said, softly.

She knew he was joking, and she tried not to give in to it, but she couldn't help herself. Faith grinned as she playfully nudged his side. "Don't flatter yourself."

Her retort made him laugh out loud, and the deep sound of his laughter was like a healing balm to her rattled nerves.

"Look, I know it probably feels like the end of the world, but I promise it's not," he said. "This tractor is obviously very old, and I think it's served its purpose. Don't you?"

She glanced at the broken-down heap of metal and sighed as she thought back to the many times she'd ridden on the tractor with her grandfather while he worked in the field. He taught her how to drive it when she was thirteen years old, and it held a lot of wonderful memories from her childhood.

"The week before my grandfather passed away, I drove the tractor for him because he was too feeble to do it himself. I worked all day in the field, and I can still remember seeing the big smile on his face as he stood beside the fence and watched. He looked so proud."

David reached over and grabbed her hand, which caught her by surprise, but in a good way. Holding his hand felt like the most natural thing in the world. It felt *right*.

"I know I wasn't fortunate enough to have met him, but I have no doubt he was very proud of you," he replied. "And who knows, we might be able to repair the engine. Don't lose hope just yet."

Faith furrowed a brow. "Don't you mean *I* might be able to fix it? I don't think *we* would be able to accomplish much living in two separate towns."

He didn't answer immediately, but when he brought her hand to his lips and gently kissed her fingers, she felt a glimmer of hope stir deep inside her.

"I've been doing a lot of thinking the past few days, and I feel like this is where I belong. I know how strong-willed you are, and I admire that about you, but I want to be here for you, Faith. I was actually coming here to tell you that."

The small flicker of hope she felt began to diminish. "David, I appreciate you wanting to help, but you don't have to save me. I can manage the farm on my own."

He shook his head. "No, I think you misunderstood what I meant."

Before she could question him further, David leaned in close and pressed his lips to hers. It took only a few seconds, but she felt the impact from it through every nerve in her body. He kissed her again, but this one lasted much longer, and when he released her, she gripped his arm to remain upright.

"I don't want to just help you, Faith. I want us to be *together*. I'll understand if you want to take things slow, but please don't ask me to leave you because I don't think I have the strength to do that."

His voice was low and deep and his breath was hot against her skin. It was an intoxicating sensation that quickened her pulse and made her head swoon, and it was unlike anything she'd ever felt before.

"But what about your job?" she asked. "I would hate to see you give that up."

He smiled as she traced her jawline with his fingertips. "My boss is good friends with the fire captain here in Dayton. I'm sure he would put in a good word for me if I asked."

It took every ounce of strength she had, but Faith pulled away from him so she could focus on him without being distracted by his lips and the heat emanating from his body.

"But you left the faith, David."

He frowned as he sat up straight and looked up at the sky. She hated to bring it up, but if they were going to be together, they had to face the fact that it might not go as smoothly as they hoped.

"I've been thinking a lot about that too. I was young and foolish when I left, but now that I'm older and wiser I realize what I've been missing out on. I didn't think I would ever miss this way of life, but I do. I've felt more grounded and at peace since I've been here than I have in a very long time. I'm hoping the Bishop and elders will agree when I speak to them about it."

It made her heart soar hearing him profess his faith and his desire to return to it, especially since she understood the risk he was taking.

Faith placed her hand against his cheek and when he turned to face her, she pulled him close and pressed her lips firmly against his. It was a bold move, and one she'd never dreamed of taking before, but he seemed pleasantly surprised by the way he deepened their kiss. When they parted, they were both breathless.

"So...do you think I stand a chance with your family, or will your brothers give me the third degree and make me jump through hoops before they let me court you?"

Faith laughed. She hadn't considered what her family might think of their relationship, but she wasn't too concerned about it. If she'd learned anything since inheriting her grandfather's estate, it was that she was capable of making her own decisions and forging her own way in life. If they accepted David into the family, that would be wonderful, but if they refused, she still wouldn't let that deter their plans.

"Oh, I'm certain you can hold your own against my brothers, but I'll put my foot down if they give you any trouble. I know how to handle them."

David grinned as he wrapped his arms around her waist and carefully lowered her to the ground. "I don't doubt that at all."

As he softly kissed her cheeks, her nose, and her closed eyelids, Faith sighed contentedly while enjoying the whisper of his warm breath against her skin. After what felt like an eternity, God was finally bringing together the missing pieces of her life...and she couldn't wait to find out what He had in store for her future.